A. FRANK SMITH, JR. LIBRARY
Southwestern University
Georgetown, Texas 78620

W9-AFH-187

DATE DUE

Demco No. 62-0549

WITHDRAWN

HEART OF NAOSAQUA

HEART OF NAOSAQUA

Katherine Von Ahnen

Illustrations by
Paulette Livers Lambert

ROBERTS RINEHART PUBLISHERS
BOULDER, COLORADO
in cooperation with
THE COUNCIL FOR INDIAN EDUCATION

Copyright © 1996 by Katherine von Ahnen

Illustrations © 1996 by Paulette Livers Lambert

ISBN 1-57098-010-1

Published by
Roberts Rinehart Publishers
5455 Spine Road
Boulder, Colorado 80301

Distributed in the
U.S. and Canada by
Publishers Group West

Contents

The Council for Indian Education Series

THE COUNCIL FOR INDIAN EDUCATION is a non-profit organization devoted to teacher training and to the publication of materials to aid in Indian education. All books are selected by an Indian editorial board and are approved for use with Indian children. Proceeds are used for the publication of more books for Indian children. Roberts Rinehart Publishers copublishes select manuscripts to aid the Council for Indian Education in the distribution of these books to wider markets, to aid in the production of books, and to support the Council's educational programs.

EDITORIAL BOARD FOR

HEART ᵒF NAᵒSAQUA

Hap Gilliland, *Chairman*

Sharon Many Beads Bowers, *Assiniboine-Haida*

Rosalie BearCrane, *Crow*

Sally Old Coyote, *Crow*

Robert LaFountain, *Chippewa*

Marie Reyhner, *Navajo*

Elaine Allery, *Chippewa-Cree*

William Sprint, *Crow*

Joe Cooper, *Yurok*

Gary Dollarhide, *Cherokee*

Julia Munoz Bradford, *Hispanic-Lakota*

Mary Therese One Bear, *Cheyenne*

Gail TallWhiteMan, *Northern Cheyenne*

Rita McFadyean, *Blackfeet-Cree*

Rachel Strange Owl, *Northern Cheyenne*

Kay Streeter, *Sioux*

Diane Bakun, *Alaska*

Dolores Wing

Jon Reyhner, *Indian Education Specialist*

Elizabeth Clark, *Secretary of the Board*

WISCONSIN

WISCONSIN RIVER

MISSISSIPPI RIVER

LAKE MICHIGAN

ROCK RIVER

FOX RIVER

IOWA

ILLINOIS

INDIANA

PEORIA LAKE

MISSISSIPPI RIVER

ILLINOIS RIVER

SAUKINEK,
*LOCATED AT JUNCTURE OF
MISSISSIPPI AND ROCK RIVERS*

WILLIAM HENRY HARRISON'S
FRAUDELENT PURCHASE
FROM THE SAUK TRIBE
(ABOUT 51 MILLION ACRES)

Introduction

The Mesquakies are a unique tribe of American Indians. They are of the most ancient Algonquin stock. Their language, legends and lore show less influence from the white people than almost any other Indian group. The Red Earth people, as the Mesquakies call themselves, were born on the East Coast around the area of Rhode Island. They are related to the Sauk and the Fox.

By the 1730s the Mesquakies, along with Sauk and Fox, had established villages jointly down the Mississippi at Prairie de Chien, Dubuque, Rock Island, and almost to St. Louis.

By the early 1800s, Saukinek, located in what is now Rock Island, Illinois, was a major Indian community with a seasonal population of ten thousand. It was the birthplace of Black Hawk, and the home of tribal leaders Keokuk and Wapello.

A somewhat bizarre event triggered the first important and arbitrary treaty with the United States, signed in 1804. A member of the Mesquakie tribe had killed a white man and was jailed in St. Louis. Five Sauk and Fox came with gifts as payment for the death as was the Indian way. The prisoner was released but was shot in the back as he left the jailhouse. The other five Indians got drunk and signed a treaty ceding lands

1

on the eastern side of the Mississippi in return for $2,234.50 in goods and an annuity of $1,000.

Since the five drunken Indians who signed the treaty had never been empowered to represent the Saukinek tribes, this treaty was not recognized by them as being legal. From 1804 to 1823, existence of the village of Saukinek was threatened by the white man's intrusion into it. White trappers and hunters invaded the Indians' hunting grounds, robbing them of food, clothing, and other necessities.

This situation was resolved in different ways by individual tribal chiefs or leaders. Keokuk sold all his tribal lands to the white man, and received valuable personal gifts as well. His land was plowed under and log cabins were built where wickiups once stood. Black Hawk refused to leave and stayed to fight to the death for his home. Wapello, after the burning of his village and crops, led his people to the west side of the Mississippi to look for a new Forever Place.

It is here in Saukinek in 1823, that *Heart of Naosaqua* begins.

Chapter 1

Naosaqua sat on the bank of the stream and dangled her brown feet in the cool water. A dancing Illinois breeze gently ruffled white birch trees that were reflected in the slowly flowing stream. Her hands lay idly in her lap. Her shoulders, usually as straight and as proud as a Mesquakie arrow, slumped dejectedly. She stared at her toes in the water.

"There are more tears in my heart," she whispered, "than there is water in this stream." Naosaqua was sure her worst fears were soon to be realized. Could the white man truly force her people to leave forever the only home she had ever known? "Where will we go if the white men drive us out of Saukinek?" she whispered to herself. "Here was I born twelve winters ago. And here has my grandmother taught me to walk in the ways of our people." Naosaqua knew her people had built their wickiups at Saukinek for more generations than she had fingers on one hand. Grandmother had told her so.

"I will not go," she muttered fiercely. "Whatever happens, I will not let the white men drive me from my home and the sacred burial place of my mother!"

Naosaqua's fearful thoughts were softened by the sun that warmed her face. Of all the seasons, she loved mid-summer the best. Spring had passed with its time for preparing wicki-ups for the summer months. In the spring, Naosaqua and her grandmother gathered reeds and rushes and spent hours together, weaving the wickiup mats. While they worked, Grandmother would reach back into her memory for stories of their people.

In mid-summer, the wickiups had been long finished, the crops were well begun, and there was time for Naosaqua to play games and make new clothing. There was time to look back and to look forward, and to enjoy herself with her friends.

"Naosaqua! Naosaqua!" Little Fawn's voice cut into Naosaqua's wandering thoughts. "Come and join us, Naosaqua!"

Little Fawn and White Cloud were standing waist-deep in the stream. They had loosened their heavy braids and were splashing in the water. Naosaqua grasped the piece of soap that lay in the grass at her side. Her shoulders straightened.

"I'm coming," she called. "Wait for me." She slid down the bank and into the water. Soon they were scrubbing away at their hair. They laughed gleefully when one of them got ducked and came up with hair hanging in her face.

"Come now," said Naosaqua. "Let us stop this child's play and get our task finished. We must still weed the corn and squash this morning."

"Oh, Naosaqua," Little Fawn complained. "You are always the serious one. Why must your words always remind us of work to be done, when there is fun to be had?"

"Naosaqua is right." White Cloud nodded her dripping head. "Splashing in the stream will not fill my belly this winter, but a good harvest will."

Naosaqua sat with her friends on the bank in the morning sun. They dipped raccoon grease from their brightly-colored clay pots, to make their hair soft and smooth. Naosaqua parted her hair with a shell comb, and began to braid it. Her fingers flew.

"Done!" she laughed and jumped to her feet.

"Oh, Naosaqua," Little Fawn exclaimed. "You are always finished before us. I think your O'Nokomess should have named you the Quick One instead of Naosaqua!"

They laughed, gathered up their belongings, and headed for

their wickiups. Naosaqua approached her wickiup slowly. She did not see her grandmother. Softly, Naosaqua called to her.

"O'Nokomess," she called. "It is I, Naosaqua. I have returned from the stream." There was not answer. Naosaqua knew that sometimes her grandmother liked to catch a little nap in the mid-morning. She knew also, that Grandmother did not like anyone to catch her napping. She called again, a little louder. "O'Nokomess," she called. "It is I, Naosaqua. I am here." There was another reason why Naosaqua did not call to her grandmother loudly. Her grandmother's spirit may have wandered away, and it would have a hard time finding its way back if Grandmother were awakened too quickly.

Naosaqua poked her head into the opening of the wickiup. Her grandmother was seated comfortably on a little pile of furs. She leaned her head on one of the willow-beams that framed the wickiup.

"Grandmother," she called. "Are you here?"

"Yes, Naosaqua. I am here," Grandmother answered.

"Little Fawn and White Cloud and I had a fine time in the stream," Naosaqua said. "We were very careful. We did not offend the Spirit of the River. Look, Grandmother. Look at my hair."

O'Nokomess lifted her hand and stroked Naosaqua's hair. "I remember when you were very little," she said. "I would fix your hair and you would wiggle and scream."

"I remember, too," Naosaqua said. "And you would pull and jerk, and then tell me to be quiet!" They laughed together, remembering.

"Grandmother," Naosaqua said, kneeling close beside her. "Tell me how you named me. Little Fawn says you should have named me the Quick One instead of Naosaqua."

Her grandmother slipped an arm around her shoulders. "When your father put you in my arms, I could have named you Twilight Joy, for I knew you would be the joy of my old age. I could have named you Onyx Eyes, for two bright, black eyes peered at me from the blanket." She paused. "But I named you Naosaqua, meaning *free to roam but to return to one home*. I dreamed that during your lifetime this longing of every Mesquakie would come true."

Naosaqua sighed. It was not the first time she had heard the story. "But, Grandmother," she said, with all her fears trembling in her voice. "Is this not our home? Do we not fish in the great river and hunt in the forests nearby? Do we not build our wickiups in summer and share the longhouse in winter?"

"That is true," replied O'Nokomess, hunching her shoulders in agreement. "But are we not bound by the great river on one side and the white men on the other?" she asked bitterly. Her eyes blazed with long years of resentment. She rocked gently back and forth and clasped her clenched fists to her breast. Her voice wailed softly as it rose to the smoke hole in the roof of the wickiup. "Are we not on the same ground as the Sauk, good tribesmen in their own right, but not of us . . . not Mesquakie!"

"O'Nokomess," Naosaqua whispered. "I have heard the whispers in the wind and I have told my ears not to listen. I know the fires of unrest have burned many nights in the council circle, but there I am forbidden to go." She paused and then spoke more loudly. "But, grandmother, I have planted a piece of my heart with each grain of corn, and each seed of squash. Is this not our own land? Are all the stories of the past to come true again?"

A tormented Naosaqua knelt before her grandmother who cradled her face in her hands and gazed into her eyes.

"We are here today," O'Nokomess sighed. "Let us do what we must do. If tomorrow's sun brings a bad omen, we will meet it. But as today's sun is good, let us tend our corn and our squash."

As they walked, Naosaqua thought about her father, Red Arrow. She had not seen him since the crops were first planted. A great hunter, her father had led a band of men and boys on a hunt for game. Only the elders, women, and children were left in the Mesquakie village.

They walked through the fields where the horses usually grazed. Now the horses were gone, carrying the men and boys on the hunt. Only a few small ponies were left to munch away on the grass.

When they reached their destination Naosaqua's eyes grew wide with fright and her hands flew to her face. "Grandmother," she gasped, "Grandmother, why are those white men riding their horses through our corn and trampling it down? Why are they looking at us and laughing so loudly? Why do they not stay in the white man's village and leave our crops alone?"

Grandmother stood still and her body trembled with a great sigh. "It is more than just white men on horses," she said softly. "I have a great fear that our terrible destiny has come to meet us."

Chapter 2

Naosaqua stood with White Cloud at the edge of the clearing. They carried buckets made from birch bark, which they hoped to fill with berries. They were waiting for Little Fawn.

"Little Fawn is always the last one to appear," complained White Cloud. "I wish she would learn to hurry."

"Hush," said Naosaqua. "Do not let such thoughts escape your tongue, lest she stumble on a rock and hurt herself. In truth, it is you and I who are early."

"Early it is," agreed White Cloud. "The sun is scarce up, and the grass is still wet with the night. Why do we always have to gather berries when the sun has but one eye opened?"

Naosaqua smiled at her friend. "White Cloud," she said, "you know as well as I that berries are cool and sweet in the freshness of early morning. Would you fill your bucket with berries that are trying to shrink from the sun? What would your Nena say?"

White Cloud frowned just as Little Fawn came into view, swinging her birch bucket and calling to them.

"I had to hold Little Brother," she said. "He is very cross and cries a lot. He does not want me to hold him, and he does not want me to put him down. I do not think he knows what he wants!" Little Fawn was not in a very good mood.

"I wish that I had a small one to hold," said Naosaqua. "I would not care what he did. I would make him laugh with the feathers on his rattle."

"Not if he threw the rattle at you like Watomie did to me," Little Fawn declared.

Naosaqua put her hand on Little Fawn's arm. "Your wickiup is blessed with young brothers and sisters. You should be grateful to the Great Spirit."

"In truth, I am," Little Fawn groaned. "But it's not easy being the oldest!"

Naosaqua laughed at her friend. "Let your mind dwell on this," she said. "They will grow up one day, and be just like you."

The three girls turned and headed for the distant thicket where the dark blue berries hung heavily on the bushes. White Cloud looked at Naosaqua. "Do you really wish you had brothers and sisters?" she asked.

Naosaqua thought before she answered. "It is not my fate to have brothers and sisters," she said. "I accept my station." She giggled. "And," she continued, "since my O'Nokomess is past the age of birthing, I doubt if there will ever be little ones in our wickiup!"

White Cloud's eyes gleamed mischievously. "I would not say that situation will last forever, Naosaqua," she said. "Have you not noticed the way Gray Beaver looks at you when he thinks no one else is looking?"

"Gray Beaver!" Naosaqua exclaimed. "Who cares about what Gray Beaver thinks or does! I have not seen him for many moons."

"Why, Naosaqua," Little Fawn's eyes were wide and innocent, "was it not just two suns ago when we were weeding, that he came and rode his new horse back and forth, back and forth, where you could not possibly miss seeing him?"

"Yes," White Cloud added, "and did he not brandish his lance with much spirit, and fill the air with such cries of bravery that you could not possibly miss hearing him?"

"And," Little Fawn continued, "was it not you, Naosaqua,

who weeded the same squash three times and finally pulled off the blossoms?"

Naosaqua stared at her two friends. She did not know they had noticed. She felt her face grow warm, and her heart fluttered like a bird within her breast.

"Race you to the berry patch," she called over her shoulder as she began to run. She heard White Cloud and Little Fawn laugh and knew they were very pleased with themselves. For once, they had gotten the best of her, and that did not happen very often.

Once at the berry patch, they busied themselves filling their buckets, occasionally popping juicy blue berries into their mouths.

"This is a good morning," thought Naosaqua as the sun shone warmly on her face and arms. "My heart sings with the happiness of my friends and my home."

She glanced at Little Fawn and White Cloud. She could not remember a time in her life without them. From the days when they played with rattles and stick dolls, to the days when they had learned to make wickiup mats and mend clothing, they had been close friends.

Little Fawn sometimes seemed to resent being a "second mother" to her little brothers and sisters. But Naosaqua knew that underneath her complaining, she loved them dearly.

And White Cloud, who had three older brothers, had always seemed like a younger sister. As she gathered berries, Naosaqua gazed below her to where the green corn grew tall and strong. She could see it sway in the breeze. Beyond the corn was the village, and the little stream where she washed her hair. It sparkled in the sun as it wound its way to the mighty Mississippi.

Naosaqua thought of the smoothness of her new deerskin dress and the warm feeling of her night robe. She thought of the good smell of the stew pot, and the little secret places in the wickiup where she could hide her personal treasures.

"This is my heart's Forever Place," Naosaqua whispered

softly. "My spirit would grow sad and wander with the night stars if ever I had to leave. The prints of my moccasins shall walk forever here in happy days, until my own destiny is filled and I go to meet the Great Spirit."

"My bucket is filled," White Cloud announced.

"Mine, too," added Little Fawn.

"Full buckets and full bellies are a sign of a morning well spent," laughed Naosaqua.

With berrypicking finished, Naosaqua and her friends started back to the village. As Naosaqua came nearer to her wickiup, she felt a stir of excitement in the air. What could it be? She began to hurry, taking care not to spill her berries.

Her eyes spied a pile of furs near the opening of the wickiup. Her heart pounded with joy. She knew those furs meant her father had come home from the hunt. Twenty times had evening come since her father had left with the other hunters. She wondered if the hunt had been good. If so, there would be gifts for Old Grandmother and herself from the trading post where the hunters had taken their catch.

Red Arrow spent many days away on hunts, but he was always in her thoughts and prayers. Though Red Arrow was a great hunter, and much respected by all in the tribe, he still made special times to spend with Naosaqua and her grandmother. Naosaqua knew this would be one of those times.

She entered the wickiup. There, in his honored place, was Red Arrow. He was sitting on a mat, directly across from the entrance. She said nothing to make her presence known. Her father was talking angrily to grandmother, but Naosaqua knew he had seen her come in. She sat quietly and listened. Much could be learned by just listening.

Red Arrow was gesturing wildly as he talked. "All the furs from the hunt were better than one time before," he said loudly, "but they were not looked upon favorably by the trader. He did not offer us a fair price for them. Always before, he has been fair! We protested but he would not change his price. All hunters are angry," he said, pounding his chest. "The earth and the woodlands are angry at his offer. The voice of the white man trader is angry. This Mesquakie hunter is angry."

He paused and then continued in a firm voice. "We, the hunters, have done nothing wrong. We brought our furs to the trading post as in the past when we traded them for goods. He demanded two times as many furs for only half as much goods." Red Arrow sat silently. Grandmother did not speak. Naosaqua's heart pounded. Finally Red Arrow spoke.

"It is the treaty," he said quietly. "It is the treaty from the death of the white man long ago. It is the treaty that was signed by my brothers when strong drink clouded their minds."

Naosaqua trembled. She had thought on her father's return to tell him of the white men riding in the corn. She had been sure her father could prevent it from happening again. But this was even bigger trouble with the white man trader. She sat very still. All she had heard tumbled through her thoughts. Naosaqua knew that somehow all these things were a dark omen of something terrible, waiting just around the corner of her life.

Chapter 3

Naosaqua did not move or utter one word. It was not easy to keep quiet. In her heart, she wanted to jump up and throw her arms around her father's neck. But she knew this was not his way. Her turn would come when Red Arrow and grandmother had finished talking. There was a silence. Naosaqua waited.

Slowly, her father turned his head and looked at her. Their eyes met and locked together. Naosaqua felt as if he were asking her many questions without words. She was not troubled. She knew the answers were good.

At last, Red Arrow spoke to her. "I am much pleased with you, my daughter, my Naosaqua," he said. Naosaqua moved closer to her father. Red Arrow put his hand on her head. "In the short time I have been away, you have grown," he said.

"Short time!" Naosaqua exclaimed. "Father, you have been away for a long time. But now you are here and my heart is singing." She looked at her father slyly. "Father," she said, "What did you bring for grandmother and me?"

"What do my ears hear?" said Red Arrow. "Is it your father you are happy to see, or does your heart sing for receiving gifts?" He dangled a small leather pouch before her eyes.

"Oh, Father," she said, as she took the pouch from him. She knew that inside would be something that she would treasure. She would open the pouch later and enjoy its contents. To do so now would be to show much disrespect for her father's homecoming.

Naosaqua watched as O'Nokomess reached out her hand and laid it on Red Arrow's arm. "It is good to see my son and his daughter together again. I am glad for the new iron cooking pot you have brought me, and for the furs from the hunt. The news of bad feelings between the hunters and the trader makes this old heart uneasy." She paused and placed her hand above her heart. "This old one remembers much that is not good. I think you are right about the old treaty. How many years have our people tried to convince the white man that we had never given consent to this treaty? They are hungry for the Mesquakie land—our village of Saukinek. They say the treaty is lawful, and they say the land belongs rightfully to them. They are wrong!"

Naosaqua looked at her grandmother. She could tell by the worried look on her face that she was truly, deeply troubled. "But grandmother," Naosaqua said gently, "Where would we go? There are crops to be harvested soon, and winter robes and clothing to be made. Surely not even the white man would force us from the village when these things must be done!"

Old Grandmother sighed. "From my old bones comes the same sad story. For a little while, I have allowed myself to dream that this is our Forever Place. Your days of growing have been happy ones for me, my granddaughter. It is time for me now to tell you of our past."

Red Arrow regarded his mother sadly. "I have known always that this time would come. You are right. It is now time for my daughter to know of the past, so that she may be prepared for what may happen in the future."

Naosaqua was puzzled by her father's words. "What, my grandmother? What is it that I must be told?"

O'Nokomess folded her arms and settled herself in her place. "All our lives were changed by the year of the spotted sickness, the year that you were born. Your mother, Bright

Star, died from the sickness. Your grandfather, Soaring Eagle, was also lost to it. Many families lost more than one person. It was a time of great sadness. Many spirits flew away with the morning sun and the evening star. But out of this great sadness, you came into our lives."

She gazed affectionately at Naosaqua and continued. "It has been the joy of my aging years to direct your feet in the path of our people, the path that would please the Great Spirit. I have always made offerings of thanksgiving for your life. My only request of the Great Spirit was to see my great dream fulfilled during your lifetime — that our people are free to roam the land, but always return to one home. I think now it will not come to pass."

She bowed her head, and then continued slowly. She looked at Red Arrow. "Have the white men not already driven us from every place of happiness? Do you not now take spoils from the hunt to the trader instead of bringing them to our own people?"

Red Arrow nodded his head in agreement. "What you say is true. I remember the days of my youth when the wind laughed in the great forests, and the Great Spirit smiled and danced with us around the council fire. I see a hard winter coming. All hunters who have just returned know this. We know we must take up the hunt again with tomorrow's sun. We must have more meat to dry. Too much of our last catch went to the trader, and not enough is left for our people. We must have more food in store for winter."

Confused thoughts tumbled through Naosaqua's mind. "There are some questions I must ask," she said timidly. "I do not understand. If this land has been ours for seven generations of my ancestors, how can the white man take it? What rights do they have?" She turned to her father. "While you were away, my father, a thing of much terror happened. When Grandmother and I went to tend the crops one day, there were white men there! They rode through our corn and destroyed much of it. They were laughing and shouting and looked at

Grandmother and me in a way that made me afraid. We waited until they left, and then we did the best we could with the corn. I have heard of no punishment done to them for this act. Why, Father? Why can the white men do this?"

Red Arrow sat silent for a moment. "In the white man's year of 1804," he said slowly, "a treaty was signed by some men of our village. They were attempting to right a wrong done by one of our people. The person who did the wrong deed was shot by the white man. Our representatives were offered strong drink, and given a treaty to sign. This treaty gave away all the lands this side of the Mississippi. We have never recognized the treaty as being just or binding, but the white men have said it is, and they have been threatening to act upon it ever since it was signed."

He stopped speaking and breathed deeply. He shook his head. "There will be no dancing tonight around the great fire, as we always do after a good hunt. Our arrows must find more game. Our bellies must not grow empty this winter."

"But Father," Naosaqua protested, "will not the Great Spirit be angry if we do not give our thanks for a good hunt?"

"The first law of the Great Spirit," Red Arrow said slowly, "is that the hunters provide for the people. We will have a great dance after this coming hunt, and then," he said, tweaking Naosaqua's chin, "we will dance and give happy thanks in song to the Great Spirit."

Naosaqua smiled. Her father was always right. There would be a great dance round the fire. The next hunt would bring much meat and furs for the people. Soon it would be time to harvest. These things were good. It was the life she knew and she would do her part to make it so.

Chapter 4

Naosaqua sat beside her chopping stone, her knife in her hand. She looked at the pile of yellow squash that she must cut and hang to dry. Usually, she enjoyed a feeling of accomplishment from this task. From the time the squash appeared as blossoms and matured into full ripeness, she had tended each one carefully. Now it was time to prepare the squash so it could be stored for the winter months.

Naosaqua put one on the chopping stone and sliced it with her bone knife. She scraped the seeds into a clay pot to be used for the next planting time.

"My thoughts and my spirit are wandering," she murmured aloud. "I am here in my working place and my hands move. My eyes see what I do, but my being does not feel this task. I must prepare the squash. When the earth is sleeping beneath her white blanket, our store pits must be full."

It was true that her thoughts were wandering. Even though she continued to slice and clean the squash, a strange, uneasy feeling took possession of her. Was something happening in some other place that her spirit was trying to warn her about? Should she be in some other place? That could not be!

"I must take hold of my spirit with strong, happy thoughts," Naosaqua said firmly to herself. "I will picture all the hunters dancing around the ceremonial fire. It will be a good hunt. The trader will give us many things for the furs. Perhaps there will even be a buffalo. Perhaps my father will slay the buffalo. Then to the wickiup of Red Arrow would come much meat and the big skin."

A buffalo at this time of year would be a good sign from the Great Spirit. In the days of the harvest, the buffalo were fat and their hair was thin. The flesh, also, was in its best condition for food and the pelts were their easiest to dress. If Red Arrow had slain a buffalo, Naosaqua would be busy making clothing, ropes, and even snowshoes.

Thinking of all the food and clothing that a buffalo kill would bring to their wickiup made Naosaqua's task of cleaning the squash much easier. Her fingers flew and soon she had a pile of squash ready for the drying rack. She took the yellow slices and hung them carefully on the willow boughs that rested in forked sticks in the ground.

"This is a good time," Naosaqua thought. The red earth was almost ready to yield its bountiful harvest. Soon there would be corn roasting in fire pits, and much feasting. It would take many days to gather the crops and to prepare the beans and pumpkins for drying. The corn must be ground, and there would be meat from the hunt to cut into strips to be dried.

"Naosaqua!" Little Fawn's voice cut into Naosaqua's happy thoughts. "Do you dream with your eyes open? What do you see in such dreams that lifts the corners of your mouth and brings to your eyes such a far-away look?"

Naosaqua laughed. She had not heard her friend approaching.

"Does my friend's heart dwell upon the days when she will be preparing the squash for her own wickiup?" Little Fawn continued. "Even though it nears the time of the First Frosty Moon, are thoughts of the First Moon of Flowering dancing in your head?"

"Why should I be thinking of the First Moon of Flowering?" said Naosaqua in astonishment.

"It is for you to tell your thoughts, Naosaqua," said Little Fawn. "And not for me to pull them out of your head."

"That is a true thing," Naosaqua said firmly. "So why do you not help me finish my squash, and stop pulling so hard?"

"And then," Little Fawn continued seating herself by the cutting-stone, "will you tell me what thoughts were in your head?"

Naosaqua handed her friend a bone knife and a squash. "If we do not chatter like magpies, our hands will soon finish this task. Then we can seek out White Cloud and see who does the best in the circle of stones."

"Why will you not say you think of the First Moon of Flowering?" Little Fawn would not let go of her questioning. "White Cloud thinks about it. I think about it. We all know Gray Beaver thinks about it. I can see it in his eyes when he looks at you. We all know who will be playing his flute outside your wickiup, Naosaqua!"

"*I* do not know it," Naosaqua stated. "What *we* all know and what *I* know is very much like the eagle and the fish. One is much different from the other."

Little Fawn said nothing and for a little while they cut and cleaned the squash in silence. Naosaqua looked at Little Fawn out of the corner of her eye. She sighed. She did not want to offend her friend. She spoke softly.

"This next time, when the First Moon of Flowering is celebrated, Little Fawn," she said softly, "we may each be chosen as wife to one of our young braves. My heart tells me soon we will be women and girls no more. The days of our childhood are as the grass in the open field. But for now, my friend, let us enjoy the flowers that grow in the grass."

"Naosaqua," said Little Fawn, "what you say is true. The First Moon of Flowering will come without our thoughts to help it do so. When crops first begin to flower, when the feasting and dancing are done, then will it be time for young braves to choose wives. It has always been so. But, Naosaqua," Little Fawn continued, "do you not know truly that it will be Gray Beaver who will play his flute outside your wickiup?"

Naosaqua smiled and kept on cleaning her squash. Only in her secret heart would she admit that she knew it would be Gray Beaver who would play his flute for her. Had he not already spoken to his mother in her favor? And had not the mother of Gray Beaver already spoken to O'Nokomess? But of these things she must not speak, lest some evil spirit hear and destroy the destiny that might one day be hers and Gray Beaver's. It was not good to let her mind dwell on these thoughts.

"Little Fawn," she said, "in two moons the hunters will return and there will be a great ceremonial around the fire. There will be much dancing and singing. The Great Spirit will smile on us. I am sure it will be a good hunt this time. Perhaps O'Nokomess will have my white deerskin dress finished and I can wear it to honor my father who is a great hunter. How the flames will dance, and how the shadows will stretch upon the earth!" Naosaqua's eyes sparkled at the thought of it.

With the squash all cut and cleaned, Naosaqua and Little Fawn placed the slices on the drying racks. Later it would be placed in bags made from the skin of the buffalo. Then the bags would be put in a pit in the ground that had been lined with rushes from the river. There would be other food in there also, bags of dried pumpkin and dried beans. The pit would be covered with mats and sod. When the earth slept beneath her blanket of white, there would be food from the store pits for Naosaqua and her people.

"We will not have to look for White Cloud," Little Fawn exclaimed. "White Cloud comes looking for us."

Naosaqua looked up from the drying racks. White Cloud was running toward them. As she came closer, it was easy to see that something was very wrong. Her eyes looked wild, and her body was trembling. White Cloud reached them and stood there, shaking. She tried to speak, but could not. She could hardly get her breath. Slowly, she sank to her knees.

Naosaqua knelt and put her arms around her friend. "What evil spirit pursues you, my friend? Why do you come seeking me this way? Quiet yourself." With soft and gentle words she soothed her troubled friend.

"Oh, Naosaqua," White Cloud gasped. "I am never to see you again. Because of the white man, the chief of my tribe, Keokuk, says we must move far away. My brothers and my father are as one voice. All in our tribe are to leave! The big river will be between us!"

"My ears have heard no plans to move," Naosaqua said. "Our Chief, Wapello, has given no such directions, or my father would have told me." She paused and frowned. "Our many tribes have lived in peace at Saukinek for as long as I can remember. Even though we are as many as leaves on the trees, we have always been of one mind. We have always shared the forests and the streams and treated them with respect as we do each other." Naosaqua looked questioningly at her friend. "Can this be some evil story?" she asked.

"It is a true story," white Cloud sobbed. "Only one more night will we be in Saukinek. Tomorrow's sun will see the end of our friendship!"

Naosaqua placed both her hands on her friend's shoulders. "How can such a thing be true? Why would such a one as Keokuk choose to leave his home? He is a warrior of great honor! White men and red men alike come to his wickiup to pay him respect. Everyone knows his silver tongue has smoothed away many disagreements between our people and the white men!"

"Naosaqua," White Cloud whispered, "even as I am here with you, my mother is now packing our belongings. The mats from the wickiup are rolled, and the stew pot grows cold!"

White Cloud's words fell like stones upon Naosaqua's heart. Even though she did not understand them, she suddenly knew they were true. But why? Why must her friend, White Cloud, leave with Keokuk? What had White Cloud said about the white men? There was more to this story than the words that had tumbled from White Cloud's quivering lips.

Chapter 5

"Come," said Naosaqua to her friends White Cloud and Little Fawn. "Too many eyes are watching us. Let us go to our own place where the trees look into the water."

They walked swiftly away from the wickiups toward the little stream. White Cloud tried to voice her thoughts.

"Do not speak, White Cloud," said Naosaqua softly. "Wait till we are in our own place. Then you will tell us of this evil thing that will take you far away."

Soon they were seated on the bank of the stream, surrounded by birch trees and a few willows that hung gracefully over the bank and into the water.

"Now, White Cloud," said Naosaqua, "what is this of Keokuk? I have heard many stories concerning his bravery. I know that many honors were bestowed upon him as a young brave that were not given to others until manhood. Is he to leave on his prancing black horse and take all of us with him?"

"You do not hear the men talk as I do," White Cloud answered. "With three strong brothers and a father who is a warrior, I listen much. Has your grandmother told you nothing of the white man?"

"She has told me many things," Naosaqua said slowly. "She has told me of unfair treaties of old, treaties that one time took the land away from our people, but that was many moons ago."

Little Fawn spoke. "It is true the old treaties caused much trouble," she said. "And it is also true that today's path is posted with many bad omens. The traders have not been giving fair prices for the furs, and the white men ride fiercely through our village. No one tries to stop them. Is that not true, Naosaqua?"

"Yes," said Naosaqua. "I have seen with my own eyes white men riding round our crops on their horses. They looked at Old Grandmother and at me with evil eyes, and talked and laughed loudly."

"Even now as my mother packs our belongings," White Cloud said sadly, "she gave me this time to be with you, knowing it would be our last. I will tell you as my mother told me."

Naosaqua looked at Little Fawn. She knew they were both fearful of the words they were about to hear.

"Many white people are coming from far away," White Cloud said. "They look with greedy eyes upon our land. Our land is good. The land produced much food, and the rivers and the forests abound with wildlife rich with furs and pelts. In no other place is life as good as Saukinek." Her voice trembled as she continued. "The white man promises to give much if Keokuk will lead my people, the Fox, to the other side of the big river. The white man says this will be the last move, and that all people will be at peace forever. Keokuk has said much blood will be spilled upon the ground if we remain here. The blood will be ours. Keokuk is a fierce warrior, but not against the white man. He will protect us from the Sioux and the other warring tribes. And so it has been decided. The morning sun will see my face toward the big river. Ai-ee, my friends," she cried as she reached out towards Naosaqua and Little Fawn, "my heart will be looking back!"

Naosaqua looked at her friend in dismay. "After my father, Red Arrow, returned from the last hunt he only ate two times from our stew pot before he went on the hunt again. I will sleep in my robes two more times before he returns," Naosaqua said slowly. "There has been no talk of leaving in our wickiup. Does the Great Spirit mean to divide our people? Is it to be that some will go and others will stay?"

"What then?" asked Little Fawn. "Who will be our voice against the white man? Who will council for us? What will happen to the people who do not follow Keokuk?" She went on seriously. "Since there has been no talk of leaving in your wickiup, Naosaqua, or in mine, it must be that the Great Spirit intends us to stay at Saukinek."

"Our friendship will never be cut out of my heart, Naosaqua said sadly. "The days that we have shared are as the leaves on the trees that surround us. They have given us a special path to walk. A path that has led us to a closeness of the heart that goes past friendship. It would seem that it is time for the leaves to fall ahead of their time. My heart hurts."

Naosaqua had expressed the thoughts that she knew were deep in each of their hearts. Gone were the days of splashing in the stream as they washed their hair. Gone were the early mornings when the dew was heavy on the berries they gathered together. Gone was all talk of new deerskin dresses and feathers for their hair. Suddenly the game of throwing colored stones into the circle seemed very childish, and they were children no more.

Naosaqua looked at her two friends. She stretched out a hand to each of them. Suddenly she realized she still held her bone knife. Slowly, and with great deliberation, Naosaqua took the knife and cut off the end of her braid.

"Do likewise," she whispered to Little Fawn as she handed her the knife.

"And you," Naosaqua said to White Cloud as Little Fawn handed her the knife.

Soon there were three small piles of hair on the grass. From each of the three piles, Naosaqua took one third. Her fingers began to braid the hair of Little Fawn and White Cloud and

herself. She made a small circle out of the braid by working the ends together. She continued braiding until she had made three circles of hair.

"Our moccasins may follow strange and different paths," she said. "Only the Great Spirit knows our destiny. Yet I feel our hearts are so intertwined, our true spirits will never be far apart. Let us each keep one of these circles close to our being," she said as she handed a braided circle to White Cloud and one to Little Fawn. "Let it remind us that where one is, the other two cannot be far off. In truth, we are sisters of the heart."

No one spoke. There was no need.

Without a word, White Cloud reached out and touched the face of Naosaqua and then the face of Little Fawn. She placed the same hand over her heart. Slowly, she rose other feet. Her lips quivered, but she stood straight and proud.

The whisper of the willows was the only sound as White Cloud stepped through their enfolding branches, and out of their lives forever.

It was all true, Naosaqua learned. By evening, each man, woman and child at Saukinek knew that Keokuk had decided to move his tribe to the west side of the Mississippi River. He had been promised a large tract of land by the treaty makers, who said if he moved his tribe to that land now, they would never have to move again. The treaty makers had also given Keokuk a magnificent black horse with a saddle blanket of red and gold. He had received, too, many gold and silver decorations with which to adorn himself.

Naosaqua and Little Fawn watched as White Cloud's tribe rolled their reed mats and took down the poles from the wickiups. These poles were soon made into carriers and hitched to the horses. Cook pots hung from the saddles and bedding was rolled and slung over the horses. Small children cried. The women and girls of the tribe rushed from one pile of belongings to another. Confusion was everywhere.

Gradually, out of the confusion came order. With Keokuk

leading on his black charger, the band of people headed for the Mississippi River. They would cross at a shallow place to the other side and settle on their new land, leaving their land at Saukinek to the white man. They would never have to move again. The treaty makers had said so.

Chapter 6

The summer sun was disappearing beyond the earth's horizon. It had been an uneasy day. Naosaqua frowned. Little children, who usually ran and played freely, had stayed close to their wickiups. Naosaqua had not seen Little Fawn all day. The older women, who always went about their tasks cheerfully, scurried restlessly from one place to another. Gray Beaver and his friends had not exercised the horses. They had only fed and watered them.

Naosaqua had seen Grandmother do strange things, too. O'Nokomess had picked up her iron cooking pot, moved it from one place to another, and then just sat there looking at it. She had also picked up a beaded vest to work on, and then let it lay idly in her lap. Her eyes had a faraway troubled look in them.

Naosaqua sat down by her grandmother. "Grandmother," she said, putting her hand on her knee and looking into her eyes. "Do you not feel well? Is something wrong? Why are you so sad and quiet?"

Grandmother sighed. "Does a bird sing when a great storm is coming? Does the rabbit dance in the stew pot? These things are against nature." She paused. "Evil spirits are walking the earth this day. We must not draw attention to ourselves, lest they do us some harm. Let us stay close this night," Grandmother said. "Have your evening food and go to rest early. The night will pass. I will sit outside a little longer. Tomorrow's sun will bring Red Arrow home."

Naosaqua lay in the wickiup, trying to sleep. But sleep would not come. Where were the familiar sounds of the evening birds, and the soft neighing of the horses? What had happened to the sounds of the resisting little ones as they were put down on their beds? There were no gentle voices of the women, calling a last word to each other, as night approached. And why was her heart beating so loud that its sound seemed to fill the entire wickiup?

She seemed to hear strange noises in the night. Did she hear footsteps running, or did she just imagine it? Were there really evil spirits lurking in the night shadows?

Naosaqua's thoughts were jerked from her mind as a loud scream rang through the village. She sat up, trembling, her eyes wide open and every nerve alert. There were other terrified screams now, and the sound of many feet running.

Scrambling to her feet, Naosaqua rushed outside. Everywhere, frantic black figures were running crying instructions to each other. In the distance, a great red glow could be seen. A terrible crackling told her that a great fire was trying to devour them.

Naosaqua clutched her grandmother. "What is happening?" she cried. "How did the fire come to us? Are we to die?"

"It is the crops," O'Nokomess said, as she shook Naosaqua by the shoulders. "The crops are burning. Our feet will travel different paths this night," she gasped. "Hurry to Little Fawn's wickiup and help her take the little ones to the stream, My hands have other work to do."

Naosaqua ran as if the mouth of the fire was at her back. A frightening red glow made shadows of the wickiups and weird black forms danced upon the ground as if they would swallow her up.

The ground began to tremble beneath her feet. Great black forms were racing behind her, coming closer and closer. Suddenly, something hit her in the back and she was thrown into the side of the nearest wickiup. Her shoulder hit the ground hard.

Naosaqua's screams were drowned by the sound of the thundering hooves that flashed by, only inches from her terrified face. The horses were stampeding! Screaming loudly, they pounded through the village, their wild eyes and flowing manes evidence of their fright. Naosaqua pushed her rigid body into the side of the wickiup. She felt the black wings of death brushing close to her. Her nose and mouth were choked with dust and she could hardly breathe.

As fast as they had come, the horses were gone, thundering off into the night of evil shadows. Naosaqua dropped like a crumpled leaf in the dirt. She could not move. Great dry sobs came from deep within her and shook her entire being.

Slowly her senses returned. She remembered that she must help Little Fawn with her brothers and sisters. She forced herself to stand and staggered toward Little Fawn's wickiup. Naosaqua found a shaking Little Fawn trying to hold onto four wailing brothers and sisters.

"Oh, Naosaqua," Little Fawn exclaimed, "Never have I been so happy to see anyone!"

Naosaqua reached for the little ones who were nearest her. They clung stubbornly to their elder sister. Bending over, she pried the clutching fingers away from Little Fawn's clothing.

"Come! Come!" she said to them. "We are going to the stream."

Her words were drowned by the children's frightened howls. With each hand holding tightly to a child, Naosaqua and Little Fawn raced for the safety of the stream. A shower of red sparks fell around them.

Naosaqua pulled the two small ones along, heedless of their terrified screams. A sudden dead weight and an agonizing wail told her one of them had fallen. She tried to pull the small form to her feet, but the child would only lay there, sobbing, with her little fists doubled on either side of her face. Naosaqua finally scooped the tiny person up under her arm, and dragging her other small charge along, she ran after Little Fawn.

The pain in her shoulder ran through her body like jagged

lightning. The stream where Naosaqua and her friends had washed their hair looked as if it was filled with the blood of a thousand Mesquakies. The fire god's dancing ceremonial was reflected in its depths.

Naosaqua helped Little Fawn with the children, who were still crying and holding onto each other. With gentle hands and soft words, they quieted them. Soon they were asleep on the ground, snuggled together like tired, frightened puppies. Through the long night Naosaqua and Little Fawn could see the red flames leaping and dancing in the distance.

Finally, Little Fawn could keep her eyes open no longer. She stretched her arms over her brothers and sisters, put down her head, and fell asleep.

Naosaqua's eyes burned. Her shoulder ached and her arms were tired. The hungry tongues of the fire had disappeared. Black curls of smoke wriggled in the air. The fingers of the early morning sun searched out the terror of the past hours. The long horrible night was over.

Naosaqua glanced at Little Fawn. She shook her friend's shoulder gently. "Little Fawn, Little Fawn," she whispered. Little Fawn sat up and rubbed her eyes. She reached out and touched her brothers and sisters to make sure they were still alive.

"Oh, Naosaqua," Little Fawn said, looking around her, "is it over? Has the fire god eaten everything?"

"I do not know what the fire god has eaten," Naosaqua answered. "I know that he danced almost all night through our crops and some of our wickiups. I have not seen O'Nokomess since she sent me to you. I feel I should go search for her." She stood up and strained her eyes toward the wickiups. "Where is she, Little Fawn? Where can she be?"

As if in answer to her questions, a shadowy form came lumbering toward them. It was a strange figure, indeed, but something about it told Naosaqua that it was her grandmother. With a glad cry, Naosaqua ran to her. She threw her arms around her.

"Oh, Grandmother, Grandmother!" Naosaqua cried. "I

was so afraid. I prayed hard all night for the Great Spirit to protect you."

Grandmother sank to the ground. She had been carrying her iron cooking pot and some furs.

"Gone — all gone," she breathed.

"Rest, Grandmother," Naosaqua said, as she made a pillow from the furs for her. "I must go and see for myself. Surely there is more left than one cooking pot and a small pile of furs?"

"Go, then," Grandmother muttered tiredly. "But prepare yourself for what your eyes will see. Do nothing to attract the evil spirits to yourself. Guard yourself. When your heart can hold no more, return here to me by the stream."

Old Grandmother sank into a fitful sleep. A hand touched Naosaqua's arm. It as Little Fawn.

"Let us go and see what has happened. My mother is here to see to my little brothers and sisters. She brought food for them." Little Fawn looked at Naosaqua's feet. "Where are your moccasins?" she asked.

Naosaqua looked at her feet. She had fled from the fire in such a hurry, she had never put them on. "Maybe we can find them," she said to Little Fawn as they both walked toward the place from which they had run in terror the night before.

Chapter 7

Naosaqua's shoulders quivered and she bit her lips to keep from crying.

As she gazed upon the burned remains of her wickiup, the graceful white birch branches that had shaped the wickiup now arose from the ashes like a black skeleton. The fire had turned Naosaqua's place of contentment and joy into a place of black despair.

"Oh, Little Fawn, my own place, my wickiup, it's gone," she said sadly. She poked around in the ashes. There were a few cooking pots left.

"Look, Naosaqua," said Little Fawn. She was holding up one moccasin. "Let us see if we can find the other one." They began to push aside the burned furs and fallen framework. The mats that Naosaqua and O'Nokomess had carefully made were now just a pile of ashes.

"I do not see my moccasin," Naosaqua said slowly. "It is gone. It has been burned . . . burned with all my things. My combs, my little red pot of raccoon fat, my favorite stones for playing the circle game, and my colored pieces and feathers for my hair." She put her hand to her hair as she spoke and looked around her in a a daze.

"Why did the Great Spirit let this happen?" asked Little

Fawn. "We worked so hard weeding the crops! We gathered firewood and mended clothing. Have we not done all to please him?"

Naosaqua looked thoughtfully at Little Fawn. "I do not know," she said. "Does the Great Spirit ever tell us why he does things?"

"No," answered Little Fawn. "But he must be angry with something. Naosaqua," she continued. "Why was there no dance around the great fire after the last hunt? Why was the Great Spirit not thanked by the hunters for a good hunt?"

Naosaqua repeated her father's words. "It is the first law of the Great Spirit," she said slowly, "that the hunters provide for the people. The last hunt was good but the trader did not give fair prices, and so the hunters had to go out again to provide for the people." She thought for awhile. "My father said so. It must be true."

"I do not know. I cannot understand," said Little Fawn shaking her head.

"Little Fawn," said Naosaqua, "did not the Great Spirit protect our people? None are harmed. The village is burned. But should the Great Spirit have protected the wickiups and let the Spirit of the Fire eat the people?"

"Oh, no," cried Little Fawn. "Rather would I give up my own spirit than see my little brothers and sisters harmed!"

Naosaqua's gaze darted from place to place in the pile of rubble that had been her wickiup. She pushed burned pieces of wood aside with her foot. Suddenly she gave a cry of gladness and scooped up a small object from under a pile of burned mats. "It is my gift," she exclaimed. "It is my gift from my father."

In her hands she held tightly a small leather pouch. "It must have fallen from its hanging place and somehow was kept from burning. When the moon has shone upon us two times, my father and the other hunters will return. My father will know what to do. They will be bringing food."

The thought of food reminded Naosaqua of the burned

crops. "Come, Little Fawn," she said, "let us see what is left of our corn and our squash."

With Naosaqua clutching her leather pouch and one moccasin, and Little Fawn carrying the cooking pots they had found, they left the burned wickiup and hurried through the scorched grazing fields to the crops. Naosaqua stood very still at the place where green tasseled corn had danced so gaily in the breeze. Now all she saw was burned black earth, still showing a few red fire sparks. Broken blades of corn stuck up bravely out of the blackness, like dead warriors waiting for the Great Spirit to call them. Naosaqua ran crying into the field. The earth was hot and burned her bare feet. Tears ran down her cheeks and her mouth trembled.

"Where is my yellow squash and my maize?" she cried to the sour-smelling air. She sank down on her knees and stuck her hands in a little mound of dirt, where she had once weeded the squash. Her soot-blackened fist brought up a black straggling vine that was like a string tightening around her heart. She sat on her heels, and ran her fingers through the burned earth. She gave no sound, but her heart cried out like a wounded eagle. Hot tears ran down her face. This earth, which always gave them life, would give no harvest this year.

"Naosaqua, Naosaqua," Little Fawn called. "Come, let us return to the river. I have seen enough!"

Naosaqua rose to her feet. Her face was streaked with tears. Her arms and legs were covered with the black ash she had run through. Stains were on her clothing. "Yes," she said. "Let us leave this place. I feel a hot evil spirit breathing up from the ground."

Holding Little Fawn's hand, Naosaqua hurried from the place where the hungry fire had swallowed their crops. They retraced their steps through the wasted grazing fields, and the part of the village that had been burned to ashes. Out of habit, they headed for Little Fawn's wickiup, in the area that had not been burned by the fire.

A great emptiness loomed over Naosaqua. "What will my

father and the other hunters do when they see the black ashes of the crops and the wickiups?" she said softly.

"I do not know," Little Fawn replied. "Until that time, you and Old Grandmother shall be as part of our family and share our wickiup. There is room."

"I have a feeling," Naosaqua murmured, "there will be no more trading of furs with the white man. Already in my mind I can see angry, painted faces of Mesquakie warriors. They will never bow to the white man." She trembled. She knew blood would run on the earth.

Would it be hers? Would it be Old Grandmother's?

Chapter 8

Naosaqua was grateful that Little Fawn's mother had made room for her and Old Grandmother in their wickiup. But she was not used to sleeping in a wickiup with four small persons, one mother, one Old Grandmother, and Little Fawn. Her legs were cramped from lying in one position for such a long time. How she would like to stretch them out! But there was not room.

Naosaqua lay with Little Fawn beneath the sleeping platform that held four little brothers and sisters. She had been aware of every movement they made and every sound they uttered all night long. How she longed for her own wickiup with her own comfortable sleeping robes, and most of all, room to stretch her legs.

Naosaqua let her mind drift back over the past days. Where had it all started? Like the small prick of a porcupine's quill, there had been little signs of trouble to come. When white men came to Naosaqua's part of the village, they talked and laughed loudly. They rode their horses as if the land belonged to them. Had these same white men told the trader to give less goods in exchange for the furs and skins? Did all white men speak with one voice, and was that voice now to be raised against the Mesquakies?

Naosaqua sighed. These things she must leave to her father, but she could not stop thinking about them.

Many evil things had befallen them since White Cloud and her people had left. Naosaqua thought back to the time last shared in their secret place of the willows. It seemed as if it had happened many moons ago. She felt many seasons older.

"White Cloud," she whispered softly to herself, "Where are you now, my little sister of the heart?"

She could feel the circle made of hair against her breast. She wore it always close to her on a deerskin thong tied round her neck. It was small comfort against the loss of her friend.

"Naosaqua," Little Fawn's elbow stuck into her ribs. "Have you awakened?"

"How could I awaken when I have not yet been asleep?" Naosaqua asked.

"Night has gone," Little Fawn said, "and I am hungry. Let us stir the stew pot and fill our bowls. Come, Naosaqua. Come quietly."

Outside, Naosaqua helped Little Fawn poke a few sticks into the coals under the cooking pot. Naosaqua looked around her. The chill in the morning air was like the chill she felt in her heart, one that could not be warmed by food.

"It is good that your mother had some food in her storage pit in your wickiup," Naosaqua whispered to Little Fawn. "We will repay you when my father comes from the hunt."

"Repay? What is this talk of repay?" asked Little Fawn in angry astonishment. "Is it not always our way to share? Naosaqua, did not your father put rabbits in our stew pot at the time of the last big snow?" Little Fawn's chin stuck out defiantly, and she shook her wooden spoon at Naosaqua. "When *I* am hungry, then shall *you* also be hungry. Till that day dawns, eat! Do not speak to me of repay!"

Naosaqua stared at her friend in surprise. She had not meant to bring on such a waterfall of words. Perhaps Little Fawn had not stretched her legs out last night, either! Naosaqua put her bowl and spoon down.

"How can I eat when your anger steals away my hunger?" she said. "Let us not speak to one another in such a manner. It is all the bad things that are happening that puts these words in your mouth. It is like the pain in my heart that will not go away. It is the empty, cold place where White Cloud used to be."

Suddenly, Little Fawn smiled. "My anger has gone with the night," she said.

Naosaqua picked up her bowl and spoon. "And my hunger grows like the day before us," she said, and ate her morning food in friendly silence.

Old Grandmother appeared in the opening of the wickiup.

"Sit here, Old Grandmother," said Little Fawn, as she began to fill a bowl for her. "Our wickiup is much honored to be your resting place."

Old Grandmother did not speak, but she took the bowl Little Fawn offered to her. She held it in her hand and looked at it. All the happy lines had disappeared from her face. Her shoulders slumped. Her eyes were sad.

"Grandmother," said Naosaqua, "Have you seen evil visions in your dreams?"

"Many evil visions have been seen by me, my child," Grandmother said, "but not in my dreams. They walk the land. They haunt the earth below us and the sky above us. They take away our laughter and bring us tears. For this old one, it does not matter. I prayed my dream would be lived in your lifetime, my Naosaqua." She shook her head slowly and muttered. "It is the old days. Once more, it is the old days."

Naosaqua reached out and touched her grandmother. "Eat, Grandmother," she said. "Eat, and you will feel better." Naosaqua gazed into the gray mist of morning that surrounded the village. In small areas, the sun filtered through. Naosaqua thought perhaps the Spirit of the Sun was sending comfort and courage to her people. Suddenly, a familiar figure appeared out of the mist and the sunbeams.

"My father," Naosaqua cried. She jumped to her feet and

ran to meet him. As she drew closer, she could see anger on his face. She stood still, waiting for her father to reach her. Red Arrow stood tall before her. Naosaqua could feel his eyes looking deeply into hers.

"How is it with you and your grandmother? Are you both safe?" Red Arrow asked.

Naosaqua nodded her head. "Grandmother and I now stay at the wickiup of Little Fawn," she whispered. "We are safe enough there but, oh, my father, we have been longing for your return."

Red Arrow's face softened. "We were summoned back from the hunt by a runner sent from the Council," he said. "There is much to be done. There are serious things to be decided. Come. Follow me." He turned and strode toward the small stream. Naosaqua followed two paces behind him. She hurried to keep up. Upon reaching the stream, her father turned to her and said, "Sit." Naosaqua sank slowly to the ground, and looked up at her father.

For a moment, he did not speak but gazed at the waters of the small stream. Naosaqua watched as he turned slowly towards her and spoke. "My little Naosaqua," he said tenderly. "You who have known only the happy days of childhood, have endured much with the burning of our crops and our village. When the runner reached us with the terrible news of the fire, I was much afraid as he declared all wickiups in our part of the village had burned to the ground. But he assured me none of our people had been injured — only the crops and the wickiups."

Red Arrow paused and then went on slowly. "We have seen what happened to the land sold by Keokuk to the white man. Where wickiups once stood, the ground was turned under with the white man's plow, and log cabins were built. We were all deceived into thinking the piece of ground that was once Keokuk's tribal home would keep the white man happy. It is not to be that way."

He stopped speaking and sat beside Naosaqua. "The white

man means for us to move further, lest by accident he treads on us." He took Naosaqua's hand in his and looked at her seriously. "It is not by accident he tramples down the sacred graves and pushes us from our home. There is only a small amount of food left in our storage pits. With our harvest burned, there is no way to replenish it. We brought back only a few muskrats and beavers. A few more days would have seen a buffalo kill. . . ." Red Arrow's voice trailed off.

"What has happened to make our days and nights run crooked?" Naosaqua whispered to her father. "Does my mother not look down upon me from the trail of the night stars? Have I not pleased her spirit?"

Red Arrow reached out and took her hand in his. "You have done all a loving daughter should do," he said. "There is no fault in you. It is the white man — he is hungry for our land and if he cannot buy it from us as he did with Keokuk, then he will try to take it through other means that are evil."

Naosaqua gazed at her father. Never had she heard such words!

"I tell you this, my Naosaqua, my daughter," Red Arrow continued, "we shall not be separated. Whatever happens, remember that." He rose and stood looking down on her for a moment. "All the chiefs and warriors and hunters have spoken together. There will be a big Council Fire this night. Much will be decided. Black Hawk will speak, and Keokuk has returned to us from his new home across the big river to offer his advice. When the drum sounds its calling, see to it that you and Old Grandmother are in the outer reaches of the circle so that you may hear all, and be prepared for what is to come." He turned and walked slowly away from where Naosaqua sat by the side of the small stream.

Naosaqua stared after the retreating figure of her father. Never did she remember being summoned to a Council Fire before! What would happen, Naosaqua wondered. What would their tomorrows bring? Her eyes filled with tears and her chin quivered. "I must remember what my father said," she reminded herself. "We will not be separated. We will stay together. My father said this. It must be so."

Naosaqua gazed into the little stream. She felt as if her life was slipping by even faster than the little twigs being carried away in the current.

Chapter 9

The last rays of the sun touched what was left of Saukinek. The day was coming to an end. Naosaqua could hear the deep throbbing of their council drums. They matched the rhythm of her own heart beat, and the heartbeat of every Mesquakie Indian. In truth, the drums were the heartbeat of her people, and the innermost core of every ceremonial.

Long before the Chiefs, and the Warriors, and the Medicine Men would take their place around the ceremonial fire, the drums sent out their message to all the people, and all hearts beat in accord.

A large circle in the village had been swept and prepared for the purpose of dancing. The ceremonial fire was smoldering, waiting to be fanned into dancing flames by the leaping figures of the braves.

"This is not the ceremonial my heart looked to," Naosaqua said to herself as she listened to the drums. Seeking a quiet time alone, she had retreated to the secret place of the willows.

"Gone is my white deerskin dress I would have worn to honor my father. Here I am, with my feet in the moccasins of Little Fawn and no path to set them upon. The drums of the council fire invite me to show myself. I feel I shall look poor in the eyes of the Great Spirit."

The branches of the willow trees parted, and Little Fawn stepped through them. "Is this place for one alone, or am I welcome here?" she said softly.

Naosaqua reached out her hand to her friend. "It is your place and my place," she said. "Just as it used to be White Cloud's place, and is today. I feel my heart beating louder even than the council drums. I am afraid of what decisions will be made round the great fire, yet something whispers to me it would be well to listen."

Naosaqua sat beneath the willows, holding Little Fawn's hands, troubled eyes looking into troubled eyes.

Little Fawn spoke. "I fear to go forever into the land where we have only visited when on hunts with the great hunters. Yet I also fear to stay here for there is much evil now about this place. When I put my two fears together, they do no make one good thing. They only make one big fear that is bigger than I am."

"To leave here would be to leave the spirit of my mother behind me," Naosaqua said sadly. "She has been much in my thoughts lately. I feel her reaching out to take hold of me. Does that mean we should not leave the sacred burial grounds, or does that mean that I am soon to join her?"

A cry of despair escaped Little Fawn. "Do not voice such thoughts, Naosaqua! Not even here, in our secret place. Once you set your mind on the trail of the night stars, your feet are soon to follow. Cover your bad thoughts with one of gladness. If we are forced to leave Saukinek, our paths may cross once more with White Cloud!"

"You are right, Little Fawn," said Naosaqua. "My heart rejoices that I have such a friend as you to steer me to good thoughts. Come," she continued. "It is time. Let us find O'Nokomess and present ourselves at the Council Fire."

O'Nokomess was waiting in the opening of Little Fawn's wickiup. "Come, Old Grandmother," said Naosaqua, as she reached out her hand to her. "It is time. My father would be shamed if we were not in our appointed place this night. The

Great Spirit will show no concern for our destiny if we do not show the first concern."

Old Grandmother smiled at her. It was the first time she had smiled in many days. "The earth has turned around," she said. "Was it not I who used to council you, my little one? And is it not you who now council Old Grandmother with words of wisdom? Ai-ee, you are truly the joy of my old age."

Naosaqua smiled, too, and led the way to listen to the Headmen of Saukinek.

The most prominent places at the ceremony were given to the Chiefs, Warriors, and Medicine Men. They sat in a half-circle, allowing enough room for the dancers to perform in a full circle around the great fire. The vibrating sound of the drum was now accompanied by several braves, who danced slowly around the circle, shaking ceremonial rattles. Their shrill voices pierced the night air as they entreated the spirits of the ancient departed to look down upon all.

The wisest of all the headmen sent the smoke of the pipe up to the dark heavens to gain the attention of the Great Spirit. The throb of the drums and the chanting of the dancers echoed out over Saukinek. Naosaqua watched the whirling figures as they danced the Mesquakie Stomp Dance. Of all the dances, this was her favorite.

The bear-claw necklaces and the bells and the beautiful feathered headpieces seemed to whirl in a never-ending circle. No other Indian could perform this dance as it was a style all the Mesquakie's own.

Dancing to the sounds of near defeat, the braves were bent almost double. Their arms hung limply, and their feet dragged in the dust. As the drums and the rattles picked up speed, so did the dancers. At the end of the dance they were portraying their great victory, dancing erect and proud, with their arms waving, and their feet stomping out their joy.

Finally, the dancers stopped and everyone was very quiet. After a long silence, Black Hawk rose and began to speak.

His voice fell like thunder, and lightning seemed to flash from his eyes.

"Headmen, chiefs, braves, and warriors. For more than a hundred winters out nation has been a powerful, happy, and united people. The woods and prairies teem with game suitable to our enjoyment. The rivers are alive with the best kinds of fish. The soil produces fruits in abundance, and other kinds of food in great quantity. Our children were never known to cry of hunger. Now an evil day befalls us. The Long Guns claim our ancient village, where all of us were born, and where the bones of the ancient dead sleep."

Black Hawk paused and glared around him. He shook his fist high above his head and continued. "Shall the descendants of our ancestors stand idly by and suffer this sacrilege? Let us send the guilty spirits of the white man to their place of endless punishment. Let us hurl the deadly arrow and fatal tomahawk into the heart of the pale-faced invader! The spirit of my father is beckoning me on! I shall lead our brave warriors and avenge all these wrongs!"

Black Hawk ceased to speak. He stood majestically for a moment, and then strode to his place and sat down.

Naosaqua began to tremble. Everyone within the range of Black Hawk's voice was howling in agreement. The warriors were shaking their feathered lances in the air. Naosaqua wanted to jump up and run away.

Old Grandmother reached over and put her hand on Naosaqua's arm reassuringly.

Keokuk now stood by the fire. Calmly he waited for the noise to stop. Slowly he began to speak. His voice was not loud like the voice of Black Hawk, but it rang clear and true to all the people.

"Headmen, chiefs, braves and warriors all! I have heard a mighty demand to be led forth on the warpath. The Long Guns are as plentiful as trees in the forest, and their soldiers like grass on the prairies. They carry the talking thunder. We will fall with our faces to the enemy. We shall only wreak vengeance upon their hated heads. If we go upon the long trail that has no turn, who then will provide for our wives and our children, our old and infirm? We cannot take them with us. Dare we leave them behind to the white men?"

A solemn stillness settled over the gathering. Keokuk's voice was like a bird song, speaking to them of all their days past and all their days yet to be. He stretched out his hands to his people, and continued.

"There are not enough of us to fight. There are too many of us to die! If you persist in following Black Hawk on the warpath, then indeed, do I bid you farewell!"

The howling braves had been quieted and angry chiefs were stilled. With great dignity, Keokuk took his seat. For awhile, all sat in silence.

Naosaqua watched as Chief Wapello, the leader of her own tribe, took his place in the light of the Council Fire. The firelight glinted on a large, round, golden medal he wore around his neck on a leather thong. His shoulders were covered by a fur piece from which eagle feathers hung. A large bear-claw necklace rested on the fur piece. His head was wrapped in a beaded red turban, and feathers adorned the roach of his hair that protruded from it. His robes hung from under the fur piece and in his hand he carried the staff of a chief. Wapello looked around at all the Mesquakie gathered there. He spoke slowly and firmly.

"I remember when Wiskonsan was ours and we sold it to the white man. Dubuque was once ours, and we sold it also. Have we, the first holders of this region, no hold on its history? Black Hawk speaks with a true tongue when he speaks of the riches of our land. But what good will these riches do us if we are on the long trail that has no turn? The many moons and sunny days we have lived here will long be remembered by us. Do we go to a new home beyond the great river that is unknown to us? Or do we turn the water in the Rock River red with our own blood and the blood of our loved ones? We must choose. I have spoken!"

Wapello's tall sturdy frame was silhouetted against the flames as he gathered his robes about him and left the speaker's place.

"Grandmother," Naosaqua whispered, "What does it all mean? I have heard no decision. When will the Great Spirit speak?"

"We must wait and see," O'Nokomess answered. "The speaking has just begun."

For the entire night, the chiefs and the warriors spoke. The council fire burned low, and still no decision was made. Naosaqua tried very hard to keep awake and to listen, but she was very sleepy. She had listened all night, and now a fierce sun god rose over Saukinek. The headmen, the chiefs, the warriors, and the medicine men had gone to the long house to make a decision among themselves.

Naosaqua and Old Grandmother headed for the wickiup of Little Fawn. Naosaqua could hardly wait to lay her head down. It was bright morning and she was sleepy. Old Grandmother was right. The earth had turned around. Night had become day, and day had become night.

Naosaqua snuggled into the warm buffalo robe, and drifted off to sleep. In her dreams, she ran free in the green fields and forests, the sparkling streams and rolling hills. And then the nightmare began. The green fields and sparkling streams turned to ice and snow. She ran through them barefooted, leaving crimson drops of blood upon the white, cold earth. The black, bare trees reached out for her like fingers of death. Although she cried out many times for her mother, her mother never answered.

Chapter 10

Naosaqua stood at the edge of the grazing fields, watching the horses crop at the scarce patches of green grass. On the far side of the field, she could see Gray Beaver and his friends guarding the horses from the thievery of the white man. For three suns and three moons, she had not seen her father. Red Arrow had been in the long-house, fasting and meditating. Naosaqua knew that only when a decision had been made concerning her tribe's future, would her father leave the long house. She turned away from the fields and began to walk slowly back to Little Fawn's wickiup. She averted her eyes from the wickiups that had burned to the ground, and hurried by. When she reached Little Fawn's wickiup, she was surprised to see her father sitting by the opening.

"Father," she said as she sat down beside him, "what happened? What has been decided?"

"Keokuk has returned to his people. Black Hawk will not leave. Chief Wapello will lead our tribe across the great river to find a site for a new village." His voice was bitter. "You will help your grandmother pack. All our people will leave with the morning sun."

Naosaqua gasped. "So quickly, father?" she questioned.

"So it has been decided in the long house," her father

replied. "I will go with a small band of hunters and we will be as scouts to find a shallow place to cross." He reached out and touched Naosaqua's cheek. "Be brave, my little one. Stay by your grandmother. It is time for me to leave." Red Arrow stood up and quickly walked away before Naosaqua could utter one word.

Naosaqua watched until her father was out of sight, and then entered the wickiup of Little Fawn. She sank down on a pile of furs and wondered what to do first. While she was hesitating, Little Fawn entered.

"Oh, Little Fawn," Naosaqua said. "we are to begin by removing the reed mats from the wickiup and rolling them together." Soon the mats were removed and Naosaqua began to untie the thongs that bound the frame of the wickiup. She pulled furiously at a stubborn knot that refused to come undone.

"This one will remain behind," she cried. "With my hands as empty as my heart, I cannot unfasten it. Nothing have I to pack. Only one moccasin, a small pouch and some cooking pots. My life has become a useless thing!"

Suddenly, a brown arm reached across her shoulder, and strong fingers encircled her fist. One hard pull and the knot came easily unfastened. Naosaqua turned her head and gazed straight into the dark eyes of Gray Beaver. She could feel his warm breath upon her face. Naosaqua felt as if he were seeing straight into the innermost depths of his being. He removed his arm from her shoulder, and strode silently away.

Naosaqua stared after him in astonishment. She had not noticed until now how tall Gray Beaver had grown! She felt as if his arms knew the strength of manhood. How could he stride so confidently when all about them was tumbling down? He was only two seasons older than her own twelve winters. Her heart fluttered. Naosaqua looked at her friend, Little Fawn. "Oh Little Fawn," she said, "he surely is packing his flute!"

Little Fawn smiled and answered, "It is plain he has already picked his listener!"

Naosaqua felt her cheeks grow warm as the noon sun. "Let

us not concern ourselves with flutes," she said. "Let us get this framework down so we may be ready to pack the travois with heavy bundles, else we may find ourselves carrying them!"

Little Fawn's mother arrived with the horse they were to use. "Little Fawn and I will secure the poles to the horse," she said to Naosaqua. "I fear my young sons and daughters may be packed in another's bundle. My heart would beat easier if you could find them, and lead them here to me."

Naosaqua walked slowly through the broken village. Everywhere, her people were loading bundles on pole drags that had been attached to horses and to dogs. When the village went along with the hunters on a big buffalo hunt, there was much laughter in the packing. Today's packing was a sad affair. There were no glad cries from one person to another. Each person was busy in his own mind, with his own thoughts. An unhappy silence hung in the air. It was broken only by the bark of a dog, the neigh of a resisting horse, or the howl of a bewildered child.

Following one such cry, Naosaqua found three of Little Fawn's brothers and sisters. They had been amusing themselves by trying to get upon the back of a dog already loaded for the journey. Each time they tried, the dog shook them off. They sat now, on the ground, wondering what new mischief they could get into. Naosaqua grabbed hold of them by their clothing.

"Where is your other brother?" she demanded "Where is Wapanuke?"

Three little pairs of eyes stared at her, but not one little mouth opened or said a word. Naosaqua shook them a little.

"Come now," she said. "Where is your brother? We must find him and return to your mother."

Still no answer from the little ones. Naosaqua was getting angry. She knew now how Little Fawn felt about being a second mother. Perhaps it was not so good to have so many little brothers and sisters. One, perhaps, but Naosaqua decided that four would just be too many.

"Come," Naosaqua said to the three at hand, as she dragged them to their feet. Yellow Bird, the youngest of the three, decided that she could not stand. No matter how Naosaqua tried to set her upon her feet, she collapsed in the dust, and sat there, staring blankly.

"You!" Naosaqua cried. "You are the same one who would not walk on the night of the evil fire! I had to carry you — running — with my shoulder hurting! There will be no carrying this time. You will walk or be dragged!"

Holding the other two by her hand, she began to pull Yellow Bird along by her dress. A howl of protest rent the air. It was the first sound any of them had uttered, and what a sound! Everyone stopped their packing and looked at Naosaqua, who glared at the child at her feet.

"Am I to be outwitted by a creature of three seasons?" she moaned aloud, as Little Bear, who was a season and a half older, pulled away from her hand. He reached down to his younger sister and pulled her to her feet. Carefully, he brushed off her dress. They glared straight into Naosaqua's face. Then, holding hands, they ran as fast as they could back to their own wickiup and the safety of their mother. Naosaqua followed at a slightly slower pace. She still had not found Wapanuke.

Steering the remaining child in the direction of his wickiup, she gave him a shove. "Go!" she said. "Go to your own place and to your mother."

Naosaqua went on searching for Wapanuke. She walked a long way and asked many people. No one had seen him. Naosaqua grew frightened. Did the white men steal little children? Where could Wapanuke be? She hurried to Little Fawn's mother.

"I am much afraid for Wapanuke," she said. "I could not find him. No one has seen his small person."

"Look," said Bend-like-a-Willow. "Look, there." Naosaqua looked. There, playing away with his brothers and sisters, was Wapanuke.

"Where did you find him?" Naosaqua gasped.

Bend-like-a-Willow laughed. "He was asleep between two bundles," she said. "He had a good sleep while you were searching for him"

Naosaqua was glad all four children were accounted for. Now she had a very special visit to make. Securing the permission of Bend-like-a-Willow, she walked swiftly through the village and to the sacred burial grounds. Once there she kicked off the moccasins she wore. Finding the place she sought, she knelt.

"Mother," she whispered, "I come to you on my own two feet and not in the moccasins of another, so you will know it is I, your Naosaqua." She trembled. "Mother," she continued, "we are to leave our village. I fear this is my last time to talk to you. I do not want to leave you, but the Great Spirit has spoken, and I must cross the big river to a new forever place. This ground is all I have ever known of you, and now I fear my eyes will never rest upon it again."

Naosaqua dug a little hole in the hard ground of her mother's grave. She selected from her leather pouch three glass beads. They were the color of the sky on a bright spring day. The pouch contained beads of many different colors but none were as beautiful as the blue.

She put the three beads into the small hole, and covered them.

"So that you may know a part of my heart will always be with you, I leave you this small token, my mother," she whispered.

Her eyes fell upon a small arrowhead with a familiar red mark on it. It was pushed into the earth covering her mother's grave. Naosaqua touched it gently.

"If my father visited here today, then it is truly farewell. He knows much more of these things than I."

Naosaqua's eyes filled with tears. In her heart there was a hard certainty. It was goodbye forever to her beautiful home of Saukinek.

"No matter what land my feet trod in the moons to come,"

she said bitterly, "I will not allow myself to love it as I have loved Saukinek. In the loving there is much hurt. I swear on the grave of my mother, I leave my true happiness here, and I will seek it in no other place." Naosaqua buried her face in her hands and sobbed. "I will keep this vow forever," she whispered bitterly.

Chapter 11

The Mesquakies had been on the trail for five moons. It was the time of the Rutting Moon, when the leaves of fire had disappeared but the first snow had not yet fallen. Naosaqua had always known this time to be days of feasting and visiting. Now there was not enough food for feasting and there was no time for visiting.

"Why has this small one been tied to me?" Naosaqua muttered to herself as she trudged along. "Her eyes have never looked on me with favor. In truth, she scowls at every stick and stone!" She clutched the hand of little Yellow Bird and pulled at her roughly. Naosaqua's moccasins were wet and her feet were cold. The blanket she had wrapped around herself did not keep out the chill wind.

Naosaqua thought of the past nights of temporary shelters and breaking camp every morning. She remembered how it used to be, before leaving Saukinek, when there was time in the evening to sit around a warm fire in her snug wickiup. She recalled playing games with Little Fawn and O'Nokomess telling stories. Now, on the trail, there were new fires to be kindled and firewood to be gathered every night. She knew her father, Red Arrow, was well ahead of them with other hunters. They were traveling in the dug-out canoes, seeking a shallow place to cross the Mississippi, and hoping for the kill of a white-tailed deer or a buffalo.

A sudden jerk on Naosaqua's hand told her that Yellow Bird had lost her footing. Naosaqua paused and bent over to help the small child to her feet. "You must try not to fall," she said crossly. "I know your feet are tired and you are hungry but that is no fault of mine." She straightened Yellow Bird's clothing and put her hand softly on the child's face. "Perhaps tonight the hunters will meet us and there will be a rabbit in the stew pot." Naosaqua looked at Yellow Bird closely. The small child's eyes were full of tears but no sound came from her lips. "Why do you not speak?" Naosaqua asked, shaking her gently. "Why do you not cry out or make some sound?" Shrugging her shoulders, Naosaqua was about to resume her weary march with her small companion, when a hand was placed on her shoulder. Straightening up, Naosaqua looked into the eyes of Little Fawn.

"Naosaqua," Little Fawn said, "a runner has come with news! We will make camp on the far side of the big river this night. Your father and the other hunters await us there." She paused and grasped Naosaqua by the arms excitedly. "Naosaqua, the fire will be ready and a white-tailed deer will be roasting!"

"My ears hear your words," Naosaqua said. "But my heart will not know it is so until my eyes behold it. What I cannot see with my own eyes may not be true."

"Naosaqua," Little Fawn exclaimed, "what are these hard words that fall from your mouth?"

Naosaqua frowned at her friend. "They are the same as the hard earth that greets each foot as I put it forward," she complained. "They are the same as the rocks we sleep upon each night. They are the same as the hard parched corn we long chewed for our midday meal."

"Think on this, Naosaqua," Little Fawn said. "This night will see the big river between our people and the white men. There will be no need to break camp in the morning and hurry on. Then will we have a little time for talking and planning."

"What is there to plan?" Naosaqua asked. "When the sun brings a new day, I have no plan. I have no forever place. What

can such a one do with one moccasin? The plan in my head for tomorrow is to chew the hard corn or be hungry!"

Naosaqua groaned. "I have a big worry in my head, Little Fawn," she said. "The people in our tribe are as the leaves on a tree, while the hunters are as the petals on one small flower. The joy of my father's heart is to provide for the people. Even if the Great Spirit made every arrow fly straight and true, there will not be enough game. My father's heart will know a great sorrow, and our people will be hungry."

There were no storage pits full of good pumpkin and squash and beans. Naosaqua knew there were days to come when her belly would growl with hunger, and there would be very little to eat.

Naosaqua's thoughts were interrupted by the sight that greeted her eyes. They had reached their crossing place. The shining river stretched wide to the other shore. Naosaqua could hardly distinguish the figures across the Mississippi, but she could see the smoke of a big cooking fire curling up into the sky. She tightened her grip on Yellow Bird's hand and turned to Little Fawn.

"How do we know for sure, Little Fawn?" she asked fearfully. "It is very wide and perhaps may be as deep."

"Hold fast to Yellow Bird as I do to my small brother, Wapanuke," Little Fawn answered. "The ceremony to the Spirit of the River will tell us what to do."

"That is true," Naosaqua agreed. "Let us go closer and stand near the Medicine Man as he makes offerings." She frowned. "But where will he get the live duck that is needed, Little Fawn?"

"I have heard that the runner carried one with him when he brought news of our crossing," Little Fawn answered.

Naosaqua hurried to be with the other members of the tribe, pulling Yellow Bird along. Little Fawn and her brother followed close behind.

Naosaqua watched as the Medicine Man prepared for the ceremony. She could see tobacco from the sacred bundle placed on a deerskin. She saw Chief Sapello and all his war-riors gather to one side of the Medicine Man. She heard the singers and the drummers begin their soft, slow chant.

Naosaqua hardly breathed as the Medicine Man held the wild duck in his hands and chanted a powerful spell upon it. Her eyes followed his deliberate movements as he put the duck on the deerskin next to the tobacco. She waited for the duck to fly away, but it did not. Naosaqua knew this was a good sign that meant the Spirit of the River was listening.

Naosaqua had forgotten her cold feet and wet moccasins. She was lost in the simple beauty of the ceremony as the drummers and singers loudly took up the chant that had been started by the Medicine Man. She could smell the leaves of tobacco as he crumbled them in his hands and threw them to the four winds. The words that he chanted fell clearly on her ears.

"I ask the Spirit of the River to look with favor upon his children so that none of them might drown while crossing his waters. I ask the Spirit of the River to send no flood. May it lead the fish and the wild duck to his children so that they might eat well."

Naosaqua clutched at her robe as the Medicine Man picked up the wild duck and threw him high in the air. She watched as the duck circled one time above the heads of the Mesquakies, and then flew in a straight line across the river. She knew the Spirit of the River had spoken. This as their crossing place and the time was now.

With the Medicine Man leading the way, the long column of Mesquakie Indians plunged into the cold water. Naosaqua lifted Yellow Bird, and placed her little arms around her neck.

"We are going into the water," she said. "Do not be afraid. Hold tightly. Do not let go."

Yellow Bird made no sound. She looked at Naosaqua with big round eyes. Then she looked at the river. Her eyes grew bigger, and her arms tightened around Naosaqua's neck.

Naosaqua waded into the water with Little Fawn. Soon

they were waist deep. The water swirled around them and made every step difficult. The dogs swam easily ahead with their bundles, but some of the horses reared and struck out with the hooves.

Naosaqua gritted her teeth. Even with the fire started and the meat roasting on the far side of the river, there would be wet clothing to dry, and little ones to be made warm. Stew pots must be started, and shelters for the night must be prepared.

"Perhaps Little Fawn spoke the truth," Naosaqua thought. "Perhaps there will be no breaking of camp with tomorrow's sun."

Finally, Naosaqua stood with Little Fawn on the opposite bank. Their clothing was dripping and their teeth were chattering. Yellow Bird was very wet, too, but she was still holding tightly to Naosaqua's neck.

"The Spirit of the River is kind to us," said Little Fawn, looking back over the water. "We are all safely across and the mighty river is between us and the white man. It was a good crossing."

"What you say is true," agreed Naosaqua. "But what will stop the white man from crossing as easily? If the Great Spirit could not stop him from taking Saukinek, what will stop him from coming after us and taking everything, even our lives?" Naosaqua knew there was no answer to her question.

Chapter 12

Naosaqua stood in the opening of the hastily constructed long house. Holding the flap back with one hand, she stared at the white world outside. It had started to snow as soon as the river crossing was completed, and had continued to fall for three days and three nights. The search for firewood took Naosaqua deeper and deeper into the surrounding woods each day. Yesterday Naosaqua had not found any firewood under the snow, and she pulled down some branches from a dead tree.

Turning from the opening, Naosaqua let the deerskin flap drop. She looked about her at the inside of the poorly built long house. It did not keep the chill wind out. Five families were housed in the shelter. Naosaqua had helped Old Grandmother dig fire pits in the ground and move the stew pots into the long house. She had also helped as all the women of the five families had taken the poles from the travois and made the framework. It had then been covered with the mats and some of the hides they had brought from Saukinek. Over all this had been placed large pine branches from the forest.

Naosaqua returned to the part of the shelter that had been assigned to O'Nokomess and herself. They had been mending clothing for the children. At last, Naosaqua had found a good use for her one moccasin. It made very good patches for small clothes.

"Old Grandmother," said Naosaqua as she sat down by their cooking fire, "do you not feel well?"

O'Nokomess closed here eyes and let her head droop.

"I hear a story in my head," she said to Naosaqua. "It is a very old story, told to me by my grandmother. The story will not rest. It wants to be told. It wants to be told in the children's corner after we have all warmed our bellies with the evening food."

"Grandmother," Naosaqua exclaimed, "you bring much joy to this dark time. All the children will be glad for the story. In your head are the best stories of our tribe."

Naosaqua picked up the little shirt she was mending with her deer-rib needle. It has been a long time since O'Nokomess had told a story. It seemed as if it had been in another life-time. Little Fawn entered the shelter.

"Little Fawn," Naosaqua called to her. "Old Grandmother has a story in her head for all the children. This night we will all sit around Old Grandmother and listen to her story."

Little Fawn clapped her hands in excitement. Her eyes sparkled. "I will go and tell the children so all will come at the proper time," she said.

Naosaqua watched a smile spread across her grandmother's face. *It has been a long time since she has smiled*, Naosaqua thought. Naosaqua knew the look of happiness on O'Nokomess' face came from the joy she experienced when she was telling the children a story about their own people.

"Make tonight's story one of your best, Grandmother," Naosaqua said softly. "The wooden spoons shall scrape the bottom of the bowls and make the sound of a story coming . . . a happy sound!"

Naosaqua readied a space for the story telling. Old Grandmother sat in the corner on a pile of furs and Naosaqua spread other furs and mats around her. They waited for the children. Naosaqua could hear the wind howling outside the shelter as shadows from the cooking fires danced on the walls. Then in twos and threes the children came from other long-houses and slipped through the entrance. Soon O'Nokomess was surrounded by many children. Naosaqua sat among them with Little Fawn.

Yellow Bird climbed into Naosaqua's lap and snuggled there. Naosaqua pulled Yellow Bird close to her and wrapped her blanket tightly around both of them. The little body was warm and soft and felt good close to Naosaqua. Yellow Bird looked up shyly and smiled.

"What?" said Naosaqua. "What is this I see, little Yellow Bird?"

Naosaqua had caught just the flicker of Yellow Bird's smile. She sighed, and rested her cheek upon the head of the small child. She was so thin!

Old Grandmother began to speak. Everyone listened.

"The Mesquakie are a proud people," she began. "The chiefs are good and just. The Mesquakie warrior has the courage of the big bear. The arrow of the Mesquakie hunter goes straight and true, and finds its mark. The magic of the Medicine Man is all powerful. The enemy of the Mesquakie are as the finger on this hand."

She held up her hand before the children and extended one finger.

"The friends of the Mesquakie are as the snowflakes. Every village of the Mesquakie is filled with happiness. Children love their parents. Parents love their children. Days and nights fall according to their pattern. All is good.

"There was a time, many moons ago, when the Mesquakie village was surrounded by Sioux warriors. The Sioux warriors filled the air with their war cries and rode their ponies boldly near the Mesquakie wickiups. They held their lances high above their heads, and their painted faces were terrible to see.

"In the Mesquakie village were only the women, the children, and the old ones. The warriors and the hunters were not there. Food was scarce. The buffalo had run away, and the deer were hiding.

"The Mesquakie people did not know what to do. They

did not want to give their small amount of food to the Sioux. Then the women and the children and the old ones would starve."

Grandmother paused. Little heads were nodding, and eyes were slowly closing. She continued.

"The Mesquakie people called on the oldest man in the village. He was very wise. They said to him, 'What shall we do?'

"The old man thought. 'I will ask the Great Spirit,' he said. 'I will ask him for some great magic to protect us from the Sioux warriors.'

"The Great Spirit told the old man to bury all the food in the ground, but leave a small portion where it could be seen. The Mesquakie people did this.

"Then the Mesquakie people turned themselves into ants. When the Sioux warriors rode into the village, they only found a small amount of food and no people. 'Look,' the Sioux warriors said. 'This is all the food the Mesquakie have, and it is covered with ants. The Mesquakie people have run away.'

"The Sioux warriors looked in every corner, but they could find no food, and they could find no people. Soon they became discouraged and rode away.

"Then the ants became Mesquakie people once more, and the people dug up their food out of the ground."

Grandmother stopped speaking. The story was over. Many of the children were asleep. They were carried by the older ones back to their own place.

Naosaqua sat quietly and studied her grandmother.

"Grandmother," she said slowly, "how did the Mesquakie people turn themselves into ants?"

Grandmother smiled mysteriously.

"In my head, I only carry the story," she said wisely. "I do not carry the magic. But I tell you this: If you find a small amount of food on the ground, do you not also find the ants there? And if you take away the food, so do the ants not go away also?"

She paused for a moment.

"Can one say from where the ants came, or where the ants go? That is the magic."

Naosaqua sighed. It was a great truth. Old Grandmother was the best storyteller in the Mesquakie village. For a little while Naosaqua had forgotten how hungry she was.

Chapter 13

Naosaqua was mending clothing for the little ones with Little Fawn. She had cut the beaded design from her one moccasin and was sewing it on the dress of Yellow Bird.

"It is a good design," she said to Little Fawn. "If it pleases her, we may once more see her small spirit light up her eyes." Looking back, Naosaqua wondered how she could not have noticed the small signs that indicated a weakness in Yellow Bird. She let the garment she was sewing rest in her lap as she looked seriously at Little Fawn. "I remember that she fell many times the night of the fire at Saukinek and again on the trail. She is silent much of the time and does not laugh or cry like the other children. I also recall," Naosaqua continued, "when I held her on the night of the story telling, I could feel that her body had grown thin." She shook her head slowly. "Why then did I not know all was not well with her small person?"

"Do not grieve yourself, Naosaqua," Little Fawn said. "It was the very night of the story-telling, five sleeping times ago, that the fever began. Neither my mother or myself knew of her sickness. She has always been a quiet one. Not until the fever began to range in her small body did we know the fear of it."

"She needs some good food," Naosaqua stated, "but with the rabbit snares and muskrat traps always found empty by our young braves, and the hunters still out looking for a good kill, there is nothing but roots and a few herbs for the stew pot." She sighed deeply. "It is truly the hard, cold moon of winter. It was the time in Saukinek when we sat in our warm places and enjoyed the fruits of a good harvest. Now," she continued bitterly, "we are cold and hungry, all because the white man burned our crops and our village because he wanted our land!"

Little Fawn's lips trembled and her eyes filled with tears. "I am much concerned for my little sister," she said. "She lays so still on the sleeping robes with a blanket tight about her! Today she could not even swallow the water melted from the snow. My Mother sits quietly by her side, waiting for the Medicine Man to come."

Naosaqua began to sew again. She glanced to one side where Little Fawn's other brothers and sisters were playing. She had given them her glass beads with which to amuse themselves.

"I have been told by Old Grandmother," Naosaqua said as her bone needle wound in and out, "there are children sick in other long houses who also have the fever." She paused. "Some of the Old Ones are growing weak. I pray to the Great Spirit every day that my father and the other hunters will find buffalo!"

The flap that hung over the opening of the shelter was drawn aside and the Medicine Man entered. His appearance demanded much respect. His raven black hair was greased with bear fat, and it was braided with bits of shell and stone. He wore a fur headpiece made from the pelt of a beaver. His forehead was crossed with a band of decorated deerskin.

A large, bear-claw necklace encircled his neck. From a beaded belt hung many leather pouches which were filled with medicine powders. His long robe was covered with colorful beaded designs of flowers and leaves, as was the custom of the eastern woodland tribes. In one hand he carried the large full wing of an eagle, and in the other a gourd rattle. His face was painted in brilliant yellow and red streaks.

He approached the small body of Yellow Bird, and motioned with the eagle's wing to her mother. Bend-like-a-

Willow removed the blanket from her daughter's still body.

Slowly, the Medicine Man began to shake the gourd rattle in a circle above the body of Yellow Bird. He took the eagle wing and let its feathers trial over the body of the child. It left a yellow powder upon her body. The sound of the rattle seemed as loud as the beat of a drum in the quiet shelter. The Medicine Man continued chanting till he had circled the gourd rattle above her body four times.

Yellow Bird lay very still with her eyes closed, as if she were in a deep sleep. Her little cheeks, usually so fat and brown, looked pale and sunken. Her arms and legs were bone thin. She looked very small and very helpless.

The Medicine Man stood at the feet of Yellow Bird. He laid the eagle wing upon her body, and shook the sacred rattle above his head. His chanting became a thing of great fury, and the sound of his voice filled every corner of the shelter.

Suddenly, he stopped chanting and snatched the wing of the eagle from her body. On the body of Yellow Bird there was a stone the size of her small hand. The Medicine Man pushed the rattle into his belt, and picked up the stone. He held it aloft, and his voice cried out loudly to the Great Spirit as he thanked him for removing the stone from the body of Yellow Bird.

The Medicine Man then gave the stone to Bend-like-a-Willow, and left the shelter. Bend-like-a-Willow took the blanket and covered Yellow Bird's small form. In her hand she held the stone.

"Little Fawn," whispered Naosaqua, "Did that stone come from the body of Yellow Bird? How could she live with that stone inside her?"

"I do not know," answered Little Fawn. "but as the stone is not now in her, perhaps her little spirit will come laughing back once more to her body."

Naosaqua sat quietly, full of the awesome sight she had seen. She thought of the times she had been impatient with Yellow Bird. She thought of the time of the great fire, when

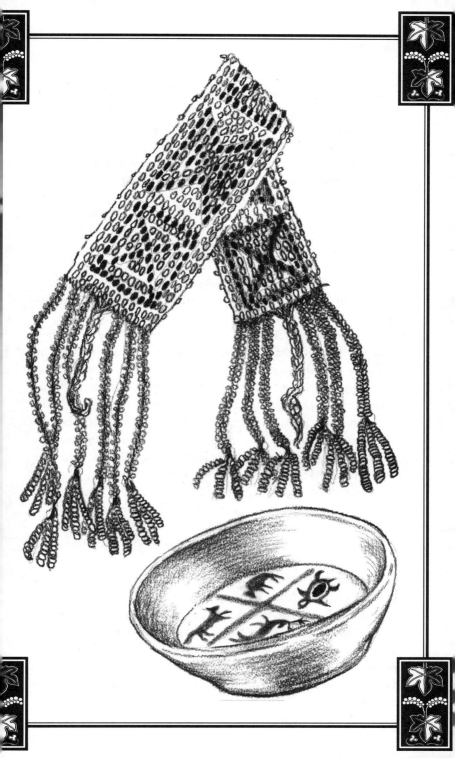

Yellow Bird had fallen and would not get up. Had she fallen because of the stone? She thought of the time she had dragged her by her dress. Was it the stone that kept her from walking? She thought of the long walk and of the river crossing, when Yellow Bird had not said one word. Was it because of the stone that she hardly ever spoke? The thoughts spun around like a whirlpool in Naosaqua's mind.

"Ai-ee," she whispered to herself, "if I had those times back, my hand would be gentle, and my spirit would be tender to her!"

Naosaqua knew she had to be alone to look deeply into her own heart. Pulling her blanket around her, she ran out of the shelter, and went stumbling through the deep snow into the woods.

She rushed blindly on, gasping for breath. She could not bear the thought that the spirit of Yellow Bird might go on the long trail among the night stars.

"She is too little," Naosaqua cried. "Surely the time of her destiny is not this day. She has done no evil. Like a small butterfly, she brings only pleasure to all who look upon her."

Naosaqua could go no further. She had run deep into the woods. The snow clung to her clothing. She stopped and sank down to her knees. Her chest hurt from breathing the cold frosty air too deeply. She looked around her. She was in a part of the woods where she had never been before.

"I am not afraid," she said loudly. "I am here of my own accord. I am here to make offering to the Spirit of the Woods to restore Yellow Bird to us."

Encouraged by the sound of her own voice, she spoke louder, and raised her arms up to the sky.

"Oh, Spirit of the Woods," she called out in a clear and firm voice. "Spirit, who looks down upon all creatures and birds as they run and fly among your branches, Spirit who takes care of all the little ones, look down from your high place with favor in your eyes upon Yellow Bird. Let her stay with those who love her. Hear my word that I will look upon her with much gentleness."

Naosaqua looked at her empty hands. One did not come to the Great Spirit asking favors, without a suitable offering. She had brought nothing. She could not give her blanket or her moccasins. In truth, they were not hers to give. She looked around her. There was nothing but snow, and the branches of the trees bending with the weight of their burden.

"I will mark my face," she said slowly. "I will mark my face with your wood, and I will fast for two moons. That will be my offering. I will let no food touch my lips till two moons from this time have passed."

Naosaqua sat in the snow and let her prayer wrap itself deep around her. She thought very hard about the Spirit of the Woods and removed all other thoughts from her mind.

She had no idea of the passing of the time, but slowly she realized she was not alone in the woods. Someone or something was behind her. She could hear it breathing and almost feel that breath upon the back of her neck. If it was a Sioux brave, she would be taken captive. If it was a Sioux warrior, she would be killed. An animal would not have crept so quietly upon her, and just stood there.

She whirled to her feet and turned to face her enemy.

Chapter 14

The terror in Naosaqua's eyes turned quickly to anger and surprise. She stared at the tall figure that had been standing behind her.

"You!" she gasped. "Why do you follow me?"

Gray Beaver's dark eyes bored into hers.

"It may be that the Spirit of the Woods sent me here," Gray Beaver said sternly. "Have you not been instructed never to wander alone into the deep woods?"

Gray Beaver glared at Naosaqua. It was plain to see that he was very angry. Naosaqua did not say a word. It was true that she had run farther into the woods than she was supposed to go.

"I heard your prayer to the Spirit of the Woods," said Gray Beaver, his voice softening. "It was not my intention to listen. It was my intention to visit Bend-like-a-Willow. I have my own offering to make. When my eyes saw you run into the forest, my spirit compelled me to follow."

Naosaqua still stared into his eyes. Somehow, she could not pull her gaze away. Her heart beat loudly, and no words would come to her lips.

"Is it not a good thing that it was Gray Beaver who followed you, and not a Sioux brave, Naosaqua?" Gray Beaver whispered softly.

Naosaqua could not answer. The sound of her name upon his lips caused her knees to grow weak. Her body felt empty except for the fluttering of her heart.

Gray Beaver laid his hand tenderly upon her shoulder.

"Spring will come," he said. "Hold fast to that thought."

The silence of the snow-bound forest seemed to descend upon them. For a few moments, there were no Mesquakie problems, There were only his eyes gazing deeply into hers and the caress of the wind swirling the sparkling snow around the two of them.

Suddenly, Gray Beaver jerked his hand from her shoulder and thrust a small package into her arms.

"Here," he said roughly. "It is for the mother of Yellow Bird. Follow me!"

And without another word, he turned and walked away. Naosaqua hurried to keep up with him. It was not easy. She floundered through the deep snow. Gray Beaver had been wise enough to wear his snow shoes. He did not pause or even slow down. He did not look back.

Carrying the strange bundle made it difficult for Naosaqua to keep her balance. Several times she fell in the snow. It seemed a long time before she reached the edge of the woods, and the village came into sight.

She stood still and looked around. She could not see Gray Beaver. How had he managed to disappear so quickly?

"Did my eyes play tricks upon me?" Naosaqua whispered aloud. "I fear it may be true. But then, what of this bundle?"

She looked at the strange shaped bundle she was carrying. Her instruction had been to take it to Bend-like-a-Willow. Who had spoken those words? Could this be the answer to her prayer to the Spirit of the Woods?

Naosaqua hurried to her shelter. It had started to snow again. The village was very quiet.

"Here," she said to the mother of Yellow Bird. "I know not what it is. I only know it is an offering to bring the spirit of this little one back to us."

Bend–like–a–Willow opened the bundle. It was a small hindquarter of meat. It was too large to be a rabbit or possum, but it was too small for that of a deer. Whatever it was, it was a good piece of meat, and was soon bubbling away in the stew pot. Old Grandmother threw in a handful of dried corn and some herbs.

Naosaqua took a small piece of charcoal from the edge of the fire. She walked slowly to her sleeping place and sat down. Old Grandmother followed her. Naosaqua took the piece of charcoal and drew it across her forehead. Then she made several crooked lines on her cheeks. She sat quietly and closed her eyes.

"Naosaqua," said O'Nokomess, putting her hand on Naosaqua's arm. "Why do you mark your face with the mark of punishment?"

"I have done an evil thing," Naosaqua whispered. "Before that bad spirit came into the body of Yellow Bird, I was not kind to her. I will mark my face with the burned stick of the woods for two moons. Neither will any food pass my mouth. Thus I have made offering to the Spirit of the Woods so that the true spirit of Yellow Bird may return to us."

"Was it the Spirit of the Woods who gave you the food?" Old Grandmother asked.

"I do not think so," Naosaqua said softly. "I do not know. I think it was Gray Beaver."

Old Grandmother gazed thoughtfully at Naosaqua. "Gray Beaver has visited many shelters this day with unexplained pieces of meat. There are questions whirling in my head that have no answers," she said. "I will go and help Little Fawn's mother prepare food for the children."

The covering to the entrance of the shelter parted, and Little Fawn entered. She looked around and saw Naosaqua. She had been out looking for her. She was very worried about her.

Naosaqua opened her eyes and looked at Little Fawn.

"I was in a private place in the woods," she said softly. "I went to make offering to the Spirit of the Woods for Yellow Bird. I cannot tell you all that happened, for in my own heart, I do not understand. I only know that somehow I brought back a piece of meat for the stew pot. There will be good food. I will not eat of it for two moons."

Little Fawn stared at Naosaqua. It was plain to see that she was exhausted. The black marks upon her friend's face told her that she was in a state of self-punishment.

Little Fawn frowned. She spoke to Naosaqua in a reproving manner.

"I cannot understand why my good friend thinks of herself in a bad way. All I have ever known of her has been good. She is a good person. All who see her know her to be kind and loving."

Naosaqua looked at her friend. Since the time of leaving Saukinek the bond of friendship between them had grown as strong as the bond between earth and sky. Naosaqua could not imagine one without the other. She touched Little Fawn's hand.

"Even such a one," she whispered, "sometimes does bad things in her heart."

Little Fawn shook her head.

"That cannot be a true thing," she said. "What bad thing have you ever done?"

Naosaqua did not feel like talking, but she could see that her friend was much troubled. Had not Little Fawn gone out into the bitter cold to look for her?

"Many times," she said slowly, "this one has wished for the pleasure of caring for a little brother or sister. Yet when the Great Spirit gave me the joy of doing so, my heart was not kind to Yellow Bird. I spoke harsh words, and once I dragged her in the dust."

Naosaqua's eyes filled with tears at the thought of it. Little Fawn sat quietly, and looked at her friend for a short time.

"If that is a true bad thing," she said, "then it is I, Little Fawn, who deserves the punishment more than Naosaqua. Is not Yellow Bird my own true sister? Has she not been given to me by the Great Spirit to love and to teach the ways of the Mesquakie? And do not I, Little Fawn, complain much to all who will lend me their ears? My spirit will not let my friend, Naosaqua, endure this punishment alone!"

Little Fawn took the piece of charcoal from Naosaqua's hand. She drew it slowly across her own forehead. On her cheeks, she made several crooked lines.

"I, also, shall fast for two moons," she said, looking steadily into the eyes of Naosaqua. "For if it is a bad thing you have done in the eyes of the Great Spirit, it is only a small bad thing. For me, the sister of Yellow Bird, it is a bigger thing."

The two friends sat quietly, each in their own deep thoughts. Naosaqua thought about the sacred burial place of her mother. She remembered the vow she had made there, and the three beads she had left as a token.

"Ai-ee," she whispered to herself, "truly my happiness is buried with my mother. The sorrows grow deeper with each moon. They descend upon my head as snow falls upon the ground. Soon they will bury my spirit."

Little Fawn spoke quietly and with deep sadness.

"Too many bad things fall upon the Mesquakie people. I do not understand why an old treaty of many moons before our birthing should take away from us our home and our food and all that is good."

"Your voice speaks my thoughts," Naosaqua said slowly. "Every day brings a new and strange hardship."

"Naosaqua," Little Fawn said thoughtfully, "When I was out searching for you, a strange thing appeared to my eyes. All the dogs are gone." She thought for a moment. "No more do they come into the shelter at nightfall. What has happened to all the dogs, Naosaqua?"

"There are two questions with no answers. Where did the meat come from and where have all the dogs gone?" She looked at Little Fawn and whispered, "I don't know, Little Fawn. I don't know."

Chapter 15

Naosaqua stumbled wearily through the snow, followed by Little Fawn. Six mornings had passed since the Medicine Man had attended Yellow Bird and it was as Naosaqua said. Her small spirit had come back to light up her little eyes. So that the fires would be kept burning bright, Naosaqua and Little Fawn went every day to the big forest to find wood.

Naosaqua stopped in her tracks and let go of the drag-sled thong. She looked at Little Fawn. "I can go no further," she exclaimed. "Without wood, there will be no fire. Without fire, there will be no life, but I must rest!"

They sank down into the snow and looked at each other. "I do not think it is a good thing to see our dug-out canoes sacrificed to the fire," Naosaqua said, "but I must catch my breath."

Little Fawn nodded in agreement. "I also know that we must find wood so the canoes will not be used for firewood," she said. "There is not time to talk and laugh as we used to do. When the young braves make offerings to the Spirit of the Woods and then fell the trees, it is a hard task for us to haul it back to our village." She looked at the sled behind them. "It is very heavy," she complained. "I feel as if we are pulling the whole forest."

"Come," Naosaqua said as she rose to her feet, pulling Little Fawn up with her. "We will soon be at the village and then we can rest." Together they grasped the leather thong and trudged on.

Naosaqua glanced up at the sky. "I have not seen a bird for many moons," she thought. "Even the hawks and the eagles have flown away from us. Rabbits and opossums do not come into the traps, and the fish have buried themselves in the mud of the river."

Reaching the village, they rolled the wood from their sled, and collapsed by the pile of firewood.

"My legs will carry me no further," Little Fawn gasped. "Let us rest. The firewood will not run away."

Naosaqua nodded in agreement. There was a sharp pain between her shoulders, and her hand throbbed where the deer-skin thong had cut into it.

"In my dreams," Little Fawn whispered, "I see a huge stew-pot. It is bubbling with good vegetables from our harvests, herbs from the fields, and a large, fat rabbit. The smell of it is so strong, it awakens me. Once again I feel the hunger inside me and my belly tightens."

"It is a shame we cannot eat our dreams," Naosaqua retorted bitterly. "Dreams are of no value. There was a time when a dream was a vision of the future. I do not dream. I only sleep and wake and haul the wood." She frowned at the snow around them. "Perhaps we are all lost in a bad dream. Perhaps there will never be more than there is now. Once our lives flowed from the earth. Where is the earth now? There is only the cold and the snow, giving nothing and taking all." Her head drooped, and she stared vacantly into her empty hands.

"Have we not seen snow before?" Little Fawn stretched out her hand and placed it over Naosaqua's. "Did not the snow melt away into the earth which once more gave us the meadowlands with flowers and grasses? In the time of the cold moon, is not the berry patch always covered with snow and cold?"

"And where is the berry patch now?" Naosaqua whispered

slowly to Little Fawn. "It is back in Saukinek, where dreams were good and days were full of laughter."

Little Fawn studied her thoughtfully. "Do you believe then," she said falteringly, "that the Great Spirit has deserted us?"

"I no longer believe anything," Naosaqua answered. "I am alive. I wake and sleep. I stand and sit. I work and sometimes I eat. That is what I believe."

"If those words are true, Naosaqua," Little Fawn taunted, "then why did you make offering to the Spirit of the Woods for Yellow Bird? Why did we endure two long moons with no food when the hunger in our bellies was like a sickness? Was it not you, Naosaqua, who came out of the woods with a piece of meat for Yellow Bird? And after eating of it, is it not true that her spirit returned to her eyes and her body?"

Naosaqua tried to pull her hand away but Little Fawn held on tightly.

"Ai-ee, Little Fawn," Naosaqua cried. "It is true that Yellow Bird was made well. Where the meat came from, I still do not know. But do you not know that there are others—old ones—who have gone on the long trail? If spring ever comes again for us, it will never come for them. Their moccasins will not walk beside ours on snow or on earth!"

Little Fawn's hands went limp. Naosaqua snatched her hands away and pressed them to her head. Her lips trembled, and she fought to hold back hot tears.

"How can that be?" Little Fawn gasped. "There have been no burial ceremonies!"

"I have heard the lamenting songs in the evening when I could not sleep," Naosaqua blurted out. "At first, I thought it was the howl of a wolf and I asked Old Grandmother. She did not want to tell me. Some of the Old Ones in other long houses grew so weak their spirits slipped quietly away while their bodies were sleeping. Their bodies were put to rest and their spirits sent to walk among the stars only in the presence of their own clan. It was thought best not to have a tribal ceremony when there is so much sorrow and sickness already on the shoulders of each of us."

Little Fawn gazed at her friend in shocked disbelief. She crossed her arms on her chest and clutched herself tightly. "I did not know," she whispered. "I did not know."

"One cannot know all," Naosaqua said quietly. "You are busy with your little brothers and sisters. I, myself, would not have known if it were not for O'Nokomess. She knew of them."

Naosaqua thought of the wailing sound of the burial ceremony as it wound its way upward to the Great Spirit. How long would the spirits of the departed Old Ones wait to travel the long trail? Were they cold or warm beneath their blanket of snow with their faces towards the setting sun that no longer shone? Naosaqua shook her head as if to clear it of such thoughts.

"Come," she said to Little Fawn. "We have rested too long. My legs grow stiff and my eyes grow heavy." They got to their feet and picked up the deerskin thong that was attached to the sled.

"I am glad this is our last trip," Little Fawn said as they headed back into the woods. "Nothing will keep the sleep from me this night. I shall dream of the days with White Cloud when we washed our hair in the small stream, and of the sunny days when we picked berries in the patch on the cliff above our village. I shall pray to the Great Spirit to bring those days back once more."

"Do not deceive yourself, Little Fawn," Naosaqua scolded. "What is gone will never come back. Just pull hard and fast so that we may return with one more load of wood, and then go to our resting place in the shelter."

Suddenly, the stillness of the snow-bound day was shattered by voices crying out in fear. From the edge of the woods, the other girls were staggering towards them. Some of them fell floundering into the snow, and tried to crawl on. Others waved their arms in the air as if to warn Little Fawn and Naosaqua.

What was wrong? Had they perhaps come upon a great bear? "Go back! Go back!" the girls screamed as they ran.

Little Fawn turned to run. Naosaqua reached out and grabbed her by the arm.

"Do not run," she said loudly. "I have seen nothing but girls running and screaming. I will not run."

Little Fawn hesitated. The other girls were rushing by them, eyes wild with fright, their blankets dropped in the snow. Naosaqua turned again towards the woods and saw clearly that a thing to be much afraid of was steadily advancing upon them.

From out of the woods rode a large party of Indian braves. They were not of the Mesquakie tribe. They rode horses that were sleek and shiny, horses that had been well fed. The riders' garments were colorful and well apportioned. They did not conceal their bows or their lances, and they rode slowly toward Naosaqua.

Naosaqua stood rooted by fear. The braves were so close she could see their faces. The eyes of one rider caught hers. With a horrifying scream, he kicked his horse into a gallop and thundered towards her. The other riders stopped to watch.

"In a few breaths, it will be over," Naosaqua thought. The wild rider and his horse were almost upon her.

Chapter 16

A split second before the big black horse would have trampled Naosaqua, his rider reined him in, and the horse reared high in the air. Naosaqua trembled, waiting for the flailing hooves to strike her, but it did not happen. Instead, the horse stood before her, tossing his mane and pawing the ground. The rider stared at Naosaqua questioningly. Even though every nerve in her body was quivering, Naosaqua returned his stare bravely.

With a movement almost too quick to be seen, the rider slid to the ground. He stood face to face with Naosaqua. Slowly he raised his hand and pointed to her.

"You," he said slowly, "Are you the daughter of Red Arrow, the great hunter?"

Naosaqua lifted her head proudly, and clenched her hands at her side. She attempted to speak loudly, but all she could do was whisper. "I am Naosaqua, the daughter of the great Mesquakie hunter, Red Arrow," she said.

The rider's face took on a look of relief and pleasure. "We have been searching for your village for many moons," he explained. "My friends and I have been sent by Keokuk of the Fox Tribe. We bring furs and much food. The others would not listen, but only screamed foolishly and ran away."

He waited for Naosaqua's reply, but all she could do was

bite her lips to keep control of her feelings. The other riders had come closer now, and she could see that they carried bulging saddle bags and pulled pony-drags.

"Food?" she whispered. "You have brought food for us?"

"In our pouches we have brought corn meal and dried squash and beans. We also have three deer and a buffalo," the Indian brave said. "When we came upon the Mesquakie girls in the woods, we were not sure; but when I saw you, I knew it was the right village. One time, at the trader's, you were pointed out to me as the daughter of Red Arrow. And this one," he continued, pointing to Little Fawn, "was with you."

Naosaqua gasped. She had forgotten all about Little Fawn. She turned to see her friend still standing beside her. Little Fawn appeared to be in a daze.

"They have brought food, Little Fawn," Naosaqua said softly. "They have brought much food. Tonight the stew pot will be filled, and there will be no need to dream of it."

Little Fawn nodded her head and her eyes filled with tears. This night she could fill the bowls to the top for her little brothers and sisters. That had not happened for a very long time.

"I am called Wind Rider," the Indian brave spoke proudly. "I will lead my horse so you two may ride into your village with us."

Before Naosaqua or Little Fawn had time to think about it, they were seated on the big, black horse that had thundered towards them just a short time ago. He pranced along, and Naosaqua clutched his black mane tightly with both hands. Little Fawn sat close behind her with both arms around her waist.

As they neared the village, Naosaqua could see that many of her people had come out to meet them. They stood in small groups at the edge of the village.

"My father's heart will know much pride when he learns that I did not run and scream," Naosaqua thought. "Again the Spirit of the Woods had sent food. Only this time, there will be enough for all. And this time, I can remember from where the food came."

As they rode into the village, the women crowded around the horses. The riders handed out bags of corn meal and large pieces of meat to everyone. Happy cries of gratitude filled the air.

Wind Rider and his friends went to the wickiup of the Medicine Man, who offered tobacco to the newcomers.

Bowing low, Wind Rider accepted the gift. He stood silently for a moment. "Let our smoke ascend to the Great Spirit," he said to the Medicine Man, "so that he may know a good thing has come to pass."

The Medicine Man swept back the flap of his wickiup. "Accept the honored place by my small fire," he said to Wind Rider. All the braves entered his wickiup.

Later, in their own shelter, Naosaqua and Little Fawn were the center of much interest. No questions were asked, but many a Mesquakie approached them just to gaze into their faces or to touch their arms.

Naosaqua sat in her resting place. The smell of the stew pots cooking filled her nose, and the shelter was warmer than it had been for a long time. She removed her moccasins and wiggled her toes in the warmth. Little Fawn approached her, a small bowl of hot broth in each hand, and together they sipped from their bowls.

"There will be real feasting," Naosaqua said quietly. "Never has there been such broth! Not even in my dreams."

Little Fawn nodded in agreement. "You are very brave," she said. "You did not run one step. From where does a heart find such courage, Naosaqua?"

"I was no more brave than you, my friend," Naosaqua replied. "Did we not stand together?"

Little Fawn considered her words before she spoke them. "I tried to run, but my legs would not carry me. It was not the courage of my heart that held me there. It was the weakness of my legs, Naosaqua."

Naosaqua smiled at her friend. "It does not matter why you did not run, Little Fawn. It is a true thing that we stood together."

Old Grandmother approached them and sat down. Her eyes were twinkling and there were happy lines on her face.

"Shall we have to change your names?" she said. "All the tribes are talking of what was done today. They call you 'Two Who Stand as One.' There will be a ceremonial fire and dancing. The other girls all hang their heads."

"Little Fawn and I will go to them," Naosaqua declared. "There is no reason for them to feel shame. When you are in the deep woods, things appear different. Eyes can see what is not really there. Had we been in the woods, our moccasins would have run with the rest."

O'Nokomess did not argue the fact. She had other news. "The bringers of food are from Keokuk's tribe," she said. "They have told of seeing a large Sioux war party while they were hunting. They talk around the fire now with Chief Wapello. Keokuk has sent a message to us to travel up the river of the Iowa territory and make our village closer to the village of the Fox. There he can help protect us from the Sioux, and our hunters can follow the trail of the buffalo with the Fox hunters. It is a good plan. Perhaps Keokuk's destiny was to leave Saukinek to help us find a new village — a new forever place. Yes," Grandmother nodded her head wisely, "it is a good plan."

"Will our chief agree to such a plan?" Naosaqua asked.

"I have thought in my head that says one moon will see a ceremonial fire, and the next moon will see us moving," Old Grandmother reasoned.

"Will it not be dangerous, if there is a Sioux war party on the path?" Little Fawn wondered aloud.

"We have a good friend in Keokuk," Old Grandmother answered. "He has instructed his braves to help us prepare for the journey, and to accompany us on the trail."

A new thought entered Naosaqua's head. "But what of my father?" she said. "What of my father and the other hunters?

What will happen when they return and find us gone?"

Old Grandmother smiled. "Red Arrow knows well the signs of the trail. He and the other hunters will know where we have gone, and who has gone with us. My bones are weary from moving but my heart sings." She paused and then continued. "A vision has come to the shaman of our village. He has been shown that on this journey we will find our true home. One from which we can roam, but always return. Only the Great Spirit knows the truth of it, but in my heart I have a good feeling."

Naosaqua laughed. "Grandmother," she said, "we all have a good feeling. It comes with having a full belly. It comes with the warmth of much wood and new sleeping robes. It comes with the safety of the Fox braves in our village to protect us and to help us."

"Yes," Little Fawn murmured, "and one of them is very handsome, too."

Old Grandmother and Naosaqua both looked at Little Fawn with astonishment.

"And which one is that?" asked Naosaqua.

"He is the one who remembered I was at the trader's with you," answered Little Fawn dreamily. "He is the one whose great black horse I rode upon. He is the one who is called Wind Rider." She considered her words for a moment, and then continued softly, "Is that not a name to be much proud of—Wind Rider?"

Naosaqua did not answer. She had a feeling that Little Fawn had already made up her own mind.

Chapter 17

Naosaqua looked around her at the now deserted hard-winter village of the Mesquakies. She had enjoyed one night of feasting and watched the young braves dance around last night's ceremonial fire. Naosaqua had danced in the Bean Dance to express a heart full of gratitude for the food that had been brought to them by the Fox braves sent by Keokuk. She had danced with Little Fawn and the other females of the tribe.

Naosaqua was glad to leave behind her the black holes from the fire pits and the empty footprints of unhappy memories. Yet the thoughts of the time spent there walked beside her like a gray ghost as she turned to take her place in the line of Mesquakies that were once more on the trail. She knew she would never forget the long days of cold and hunger and the sorrowful wail that told of the lonesome burial of an Old One.

Six times the night had descended upon them, and six times the Mesquakies made camp beside the river in the Iowa Territory. Naosaqua did not think about how many days they had been on the trail. She made camp, cooked, and looked for firewood as if it were the only life she would ever know. She ate and slept, and rose again in the morning to break camp, pack and move on. There was no joy in her heart.

But for Little Fawn, Naosaqua knew, the hard trail had

turned into a great adventure. She spent much time singing the praises of the Fox braves to Naosaqua, especially about Wind Rider. Sometimes Naosaqua would catch a glimpse of him as he rode by on his black horse, always looking Little Fawn's way.

"Look, Naosaqua," Little Fawn would say. "There he is."

Naosaqua noticed that although he never seemed to look their way, he rode by very often.

The Mesquakie braves and young boys who were traveling in the dug-out canoes kept one day ahead of the rest of the tribe. They scouted for a good place to make camp. They started the evening fires and sometimes trapped small game.

All day the sun had hidden behind scuttling gray clouds. The snow was melting into the ground, and the earth could be seen in small, bare patches. It was time once more to make camp.

"Come, Little Fawn," Naosaqua said. "Let us seek wood for the fire."

"I have been instructed to see to the safety of my brothers and sisters," Little Fawn answered. "Another must accompany you."

"I will walk with you, Naosaqua," said Old Grandmother. "I see a small hill not far off, with a grove of trees. We should find much wood on the ground there, now that the snow is sinking into the earth."

"But, Old Grandmother," Naosaqua protested, "Are you not weary from the day's journey?"

"My bones are weary," groaned Old Grandmother. "But my spirit tells me there is one thing yet I must do this day. Come, we go."

Naosaqua walked with her grandmother to the grove of trees.

"Your father, Red Arrow, will be joining us soon," O'Nokomess remarked. "A runner came today with the news. The hunters have been at Saukinek to see the trader. They wish to draw on next season's furs for provisions. The runner says it is not good at Saukinek."

Naosaqua stopped walking and stared at her grandmother. "Not good at Saukinek?" she repeated. "Then truly has the earth turned around, and it will not be good any place on the earth!"

Old Grandmother put her hand on Naosaqua's arm. "I have brought my blanket," she said. "Let us sit a little while and talk. There is much to say."

Naosaqua sat on the blanket beside her grandmother. Her grandmother studied her for a long time before she spoke.

"For many moons I have not heard your laughter. Gone is the smile from your face and the gleam from your eye. The voice that I welcomed as the song of a bird now falls on my ears in a complaining way. What has happened to the joy of my old age?"

"Would that your eyes could see into my heart, Old Grandmother," Naosaqua sighed. "Then there would be no need for your questions. I see no happiness ahead for this one. I see no village in the moons to come where my wickiup will be a place of warm contentment. Once my heart was certain in the ways of our people, and my moccasins were set in the path I knew to be good. Now I travel in the moccasins of another and know not the path I follow or where it will lead."

"Is it your belief, then," said Old Grandmother, "that the Great Spirit is looking another way and does not see his children of the red earth?"

"I ask nothing of the Great Spirit," Naosaqua answered. "I do not know where his eyes fall."

Old Grandmother thought for awhile. "Naosaqua," she said slowly, "do you see nothing good in the earth around us? Do you not hold your Old Grandmother in the same regard as in the days past? Have I changed in my ways toward you?"

Naosaqua gasped and reached out to her grandmother. "My O'Nokomess. Always my eyes will look upon you with gratitude for the days of my life that you have filled with learning. Never has your hand been turned against me. Never have you frowned upon me. You have been my teacher, my mother, my

heart! You gave me a life that was perfect in every way. I bow my head upon your hand with thanks."

Naosaqua touched the brow of her head upon the hands of her grandmother. Her grandmother lifted her head, and held her face between her two hands.

"Yet," she said softly, "I feel I have failed in my teachings." She looked deeply into Naosaqua's eyes. "Have I not taught you that from the red earth comes life for the Mesquakies? Have I not taught you the earth below us and the sky above us are the same in every place? Have I not taught you that it is the spirit of a person that carries happiness or sadness?"

Naosaqua thought deeply on her grandmother's words. She did not know what she meant.

"There is much to lament," her grandmother continued, "but there is also much for which a young heart should sing. Yet I do not hear any happy sounds coming from you, Naosaqua. Where is your heart? What is it saying? Does it not remember my teachings?" She let her hands fall from Naosaqua's face. From her waist she drew a small leather pouch. She poured the contents into Naosaqua's hand.

"What do you see in your hand, Naosaqua?" Old Grandmother asked. Naosaqua gazed at the small pile of earth in the palm of her hand. She was very puzzled. She looked into her grandmother's face. Old Grandmother repeated her question.

"What do you see in your hand?"

"It is a small amount of earth," Naosaqua answered.

"Look at it closely, my Naosaqua," Grandmother instructed her. Naosaqua looked closely at the pile of earth in her hand. She could see nothing special about it. Why had Old Grandmother been carrying it on her belt? "Say to me again what you see in your hand," Old Grandmother said.

"I truly see nothing but a small pile of dry earth," Naosaqua repeated.

"Do you not see happy days with Little Fawn and with White Cloud?" Old Grandmother asked Naosaqua. "Do you not see the berry patch and the crops you tended? Do you not see Gray Beaver riding on his horse? Do you not see our wickiup and the warm, comfortable buffalo robes were covered ourselves with at nightfall?"

Naosaqua was bewildered. What did Old Grandmother mean? She looked closely at the contents of her hand.

"I answer you truthfully, Old Grandmother," she said. "I see none of those things in my hand. Only in my heart do I see such things."

"How is it then, that you do not see those things in your hand, Naosaqua," Grandmother said slowly, "when in your hand you hold the earth of Saukinek? Earth that I, myself, scooped up from under your sleeping place? Earth that knew your most secret dreams and your deepest happiness? Earth that would have known the time of Gray Beaver's search for you?" Old Grandmother reached out and took the small pile of earth from Naosaqua. With a motion as swift as that of bird's wing in flight, she threw it into the air.

Naosaqua uttered a startled cry and reached out into the air. "It is gone!" she cried. "It is gone! The earth that you carried from Saukinek is gone. We can never find it!"

"Yes," said Old Grandmother. "It is gone. But in your heart are still the happy days of Saukinek and the good life there. Those days will never be gone, Naosaqua. They will always be with us. From the old days will come new days. From the old happiness will come new happiness. Open up your heart to my words that I may know I have taught you well in the ways of our people, and your moccasins will again walk in the path of good dreams."

Naosaqua's lips trembled and tears slid unchecked down her cheeks. She looked into the face of her wise, old grandmother. In that face she saw only great love and concern. It had always been there. It would always be there.

"There is much truth in what you say, Old Grandmother," she whispered. "But what of my vow to my mother? On her grave I left a token and made a vow to her. That vow must be honored or my mother will know great sadness and wander endlessly among the night stars!"

"We will talk of your vow another time," Old Grandmother answered. "Carry the words we have spoken in your heart. Think well on them." She rose from the blanket. "Now we must gather wood."

Suddenly, the quiet was shattered by an agonizing scream. Naosaqua had never heard that sound before, but she knew what it was. It was sound torn from the throat of a Mesquakie Indian when the black hand of death had unjustly reached out and snatched a loved one from the very heart of the clan.

The scream was repeated over and over. It seemed to pierce the night air as if searching for an answer in the endless sky. Naosaqua and Old Grandmother hurried toward the sound.

Chapter 18

From a distance, Naosaqua could see a woman holding a young boy in her arms on the bank of the river. Her agonizing wail reached them clearly. People were gathered on each side of the mother and her son.

How-Ma-Qua was dead and his death was as a heavy stone on the heart of every Mesquakie. Naosaqua knew the death of an old one was a time of soft sorrow but the death of a healthy boy who had seen only eleven winters was a hard blow. She had seen How-Ma-Qua traveling in the dug-out canoe only yesterday.

She came closer and listened as one of the paddlers gestured wildly and explained what had happened. "We hit a rock that was beneath the surface," he said. "The water sucked his body down and trapped it below. We could not reach him in time. The Spirit of the River filled his mouth and stilled his voice forever." The young brave clenched his fists and shook his head sadly.

"What can we do?" Naosaqua whispered to her grandmother.

"We can only grieve," O'Nokomess replied. "The mother will spend all this night sewing his new clothes for burial and the father will prepare a little food and water and some of his belongings so that he may take them with him on the Long Trail."

Naosaqua turned away from the sad scene. "Come," she said. "Let us return to our own place and gather our thoughts."

Naosaqua sat all night with her grandmother in the lean-to that was their sleeping place. She looked at her grandmother sadly. "Is not the death of How-Ma-Qua a bad thing?" she asked. "Why would the Great Spirit let such a thing come to pass?"

Grandmother touched her fingers to Naosaqua's lips. "Now is not the time to ask such questions," she answered. "This night is the time for us to think on the spirit of How-Ma-Qua so that in his wanderings before he takes the Long Trail, he may prepare himself for the journey."

Naosaqua watched the sun rise in its full strength. "It is as if the Spirit of the Sun wants to pay respects to How-Ma-Qua," she said quietly. She could hear the wailing songs drifting upward to the bright morning sky from the place of How-Ma-Qua's clan. She sighed deeply. The night of meditation had passed and it was time for her to go with Old Grandmother to the place of How-Ma-Qua and his grieving clan.

After the burial of the young boy, the Mesquakies began to break camp once more. "Look," said Old Grandmother. "The mother of How-Ma-Qua sits firmly beside her stew pot and all her belongings. She is not packing."

Naosaqua put down her bundle and looked at the woman. It was true. She sat stubbornly with her arms folded and her head hanging down. Naosaqua heard the woman cry out in a loud voice. "I will not leave this place for it is here the spirit of my boy is wandering. I cannot leave. Go!" she shouted. "Go, and leave me!"

Naosaqua watched in bewilderment as the wise men of the tribe consulted between themselves and then talked to the woman. "What will happen, Grandmother?" Naosaqua asked as she sat on her bundle and watched.

"I do not know," grandmother answered. She, too, sat on her bundle and watched.

They waited as all the headmen of the tribe gathered to make a decision. They made a small Council Fire and watched the smoke curl above their heads. Naosaqua knew they were considering the importance of How-Ma-Qua's death and his mother's refusal to leave this place. She looked around her. All packing had stopped. Everyone was waiting for some decision to be made by the headmen.

Finally, Chief Wapello turned to them and spoke. "We will remain here for two mornings," he said in a loud, clear voice. "We will wait for a sign from the Great Spirit. We shall smoke and fast and wait. I have spoken."

Naosaqua and her grandmother used the days of waiting to cook and to mend clothing. One morning, Naosaqua had awakened to find a fat rabbit ready for the stew pot hanging from the side of their lean-to. She suspected it had been left there by Gray Beaver. She knew that Gray Beaver and his friends made many trips into the forest, and that they had reported seeing many deer and buffalo close by.

Naosaqua watched the smoke of the Council Fire drift upward. It did not curl up in a straight line, but spread itself above the Mesquakies. The two mornings of waiting had passed. Naosaqua sat in the lean-to with Old Grandmother, awaiting the decision of the tribe's headmen. When the decision was made, the tribe would all gather to hear the words of their chief.

Naosaqua's heart jumped as Chief Wapello turned from the Council Fire and faced his people. Followed by Old Grandmother, she hurried with the rest of the tribe to hear his words. When all were gathered, the chief spoke. All listened quietly.

"The death of How-Ma-Qua is a sad thing," Chief Wapello said slowly. "The Great Spirit demands that his spirit walks this place till his time has come. The Great Spirit allowed this to happen for a reason. Have we been walking on the trail with our eyes closed?" He paused and spread his arms out wide. "The Great Spirit tells us to look at this place through the eyes of How-Ma-Qua. The river yields up fish and wild fowl;

small game runs into our traps; the buffalo and the white-tailed deer find this place favorable." He folded his arms and continued. "It will soon be the time of the Planting Moon. The earth here is good and will welcome our corn and our beans. Let us open our eyes and look well around us. Let us look at our new Forever Place. We will stay in this place and make a new Mesquakie village. I have spoken."

Naosaqua and her grandmother now had time to do the familiar things that had always been a part of their lives. They took long walks and searched the surrounding fields for plants suitable for medicine and seasoning. They found sneezewood, which grandmother would dry and then use to cure colds. They found much wild sarsaparilla with which to cure burns and sores. Horseweed and prickly lettuce also grew thickly in fields nearby. Buttercups and daisies peeped shyly from the edge of the meadow grass. Naosaqua often saw badgers and chipmunks scurrying in the woods. She listened as the red-winged blackbird perched in the greening trees and sang to all who would listen.

Digging into a bed of moss, Naosaqua discovered a clump of arbutus. The tiny pink flowers winked up at her as if to say the First Moon of Flowering was not far away. Thoughts of Gray Beaver crept unbidden into Naosaqua's mind and heart. She remembered his strong arm across her shoulder when he pulled loose the knot in the wickiup ram at Saukinek. She remembered the time alone in the snowy woods when she had looked deeply into his eyes. Her face grew warm and she clutched the arbutus in her hand tightly. Later, Naosaqua sat with her grandmother in their lean-to sorting out all they had collected.

"You are very quiet," Grandmother said. "Where are your thoughts?"

"There are more questions than thoughts in my head," Naosaqua answered. She studied the plants in her hand and then continued. "This one does not know even how to put them into words."

O'Nokomess regarded her thoughtfully. "Can you say the name of the one who has caused these questions in your head?" she asked.

"It is . . . it is . . . Gray Beaver," Naosaqua whispered so low that her voice could hardly be heard.

"And what of Gray Beaver?" Grandmother asked quietly.

"He . . . he has changed," said Naosaqua.

"In what way has he changed? To my eyes, he seems all that he ever was," Grandmother stated.

Naosaqua looked her grandmother straight in the eyes. "He . . . he has grown very strong . . . and . . . and tall! He seems to know. . ." Her voice trailed off.

"He seems to know what, Naosaqua?"

"He seems to know everything! When he looks at me, I feel he even knows what I am thinking." Naosaqua's words came out in a rush.

Old Grandmother reached out and put her hand on Naosaqua's arm. "And what is it that you are thinking, my granddaughter?" she asked gently. "Are your thoughts not turning to the First Moon of Flowering, the time of new life, the time the white man calls June?"

"I . . . I . . . yes," Naosaqua stammered.

"And do you think that Gray Beaver has changed and you have remained the same?"

Naosaqua looked questioningly at her grandmother. "Have I changed?" she asked with surprise.

"You are changing as a small stream flows to a river; as a sapling grows to a tree; as a young girl looks forward to the First Moon of Flowering when she hopes to be chosen by the young brave she loves." Neither Naosaqua or her grandmother spoke for a little while and then Old Grandmother continued. "Is it not true, Naosaqua? Do you not wish to be chosen by Gray Beaver?"

Naosaqua's eyes filled with tears. "Yes," she whispered. "Yes, I do, but I am not sure he . . . he . . . ."

Grandmother smiled. "Do not worry," she said confidently. "These things have a way of working out. Listen to your heart, Naosaqua, and abide by what it tells you."

"Will his mother come to speak to you since I have no mother of my own?" Naosaqua asked hesitantly.

"The mother of Gray Beaver and I have already exchanged looks that will surely lead to talking," Old Grandmother answered wisely. "And when he comes with a small fire in his hand, it will be for you to blow it out or let it burn. That will be *your* decision."

Naosaqua thought deeply on what her grandmother had said. She knew that was the way betrothals started. But only if Gray Beaver then came in the night and played his flute for all the tribe to hear, would they be pledged to each other. Even then, she must be fourteen winters, and Gray Beaver must be sixteen before a marriage could take place. She sighed and continued to sort out the plants and herbs.

"I will do as Old Grandmother says," she said to herself. "Her advice has always been right. Time will work it out, and I will listen to my heart."

Chapter 19

Days passed and Naosaqua once more fell into the familiar Mesquakie pattern of life she had known at Saukinek. She looked at the still wet clay pots sitting on her cutting board outside her new wickiup. She had been busy all morning with Little Fawn, mixing the new clay from the river bank with flaked shells, and then shaping six new clay pots. She enjoyed the feel of the clay-shell mixture in her hands and was well pleased with her morning's work.

"Grandmother," Naosaqua called. She lifted the flap of the wickiup and looked inside. O'Nokomess sat quietly with her head resting on the wickiup beam. "I am here," she said to Naosaqua.

"Grandmother," Naosaqua scolded gently as she entered, "you have been working too hard. You have made many mats for our new wickiup and helped with the planting and made drying racks. I hear you in the night, moving in your sleeping robes," she continued, "and I know you are not resting well."

"Do I awaken you?" Old Grandmother asked.

Naosaqua sat beside her grandmother and took her hand in her own. "No," she said. "I think it is the newness of the village that stirs my insides sometimes when I am wrapped in my own sleeping robes and thinking about the days to come." She paused. "I know that is is good, Grandmother, but how can it be the same?"

"It is the way of life," Grandmother said softly and then added, "I have spoken with the mother of Gray Beaver. We are of one mind." Naosaqua's eyes grew wide with astonishment and her heart began to pound. "I think," Old Grandmother said slowly, "there are reasons in the night why we are waking. It is not the work of the Planting Moon that does not let my eyes close. It is the bright future that is now lighting my twilight years." Grandmother stroked Naosaqua's hair. "It is all coming to pass," she said, "just as I once told your mother, Bright Star, long ago."

"What of my mother?" Naosaqua asked. "What did you tell her?"

Old Grandmother looked at Naosaqua thoughtfully. She spoke slowly. "When we knew your mother's spirit would soon leave us, it was my vow to her to guide you well in the ways of our people till the day you found a young brave of your heart's choosing."

"I have thought much of our last conversation," Naosaqua said hesitantly, "and I know full well my heart's desire. But there is a thing that worries me." She was silent for a moment and then went on. "I left three blue beads on my mother's grave as a token of a vow that I would never find happiness any place but Saukinek, the sacred burial place of my mother. Will she understand if I now take the happiness at hand? How will I ever know if she has released me from my vow?"

"I feel there is a thing I must now show you," Grandmother said confidently as she withdrew a small leather pouch from her garments. "This is meant for you," she said. "Bright Star gave it to me when she knew her spirit would soon go on the Long Trail. She asked me to keep it for you and give it to you on your betrothal day so you would know her spirit was close beside you." Grandmother paused. "I will not give this to you now," she said, "but this is the time for you to know of it."

From the pouch she drew a beautiful necklace. It was made of blue beads. They were the color of the sky on a bright spring day. From the necklace hung a blue medallion with a

bright star in the center. Naosaqua reached for the necklace and cradled it in her two hands. The smoothness of the beads felt cool to her touch. Naosaqua could hardly breathe. "My mother," she whispered, "this is for me from my mother."

For a little while, she held the necklace in her hands, and then slowly returned it to her grandmother. "I must be alone," she said softly, "I must walk to the hill. Thank you, my grandmother."

Naosaqua left the wickiup and went to find the little hill where she had sat with Old Grandmother on the day of How-Ma-Qua's death. Slowly she climbed the hill and sat at the edge of a small grove of trees. It had become Naosaqua's favorite place, much as the old place under the willows in Saukinek.

Below her, Naosaqua saw Gray Beaver riding on the horse that had been given to him by Keokuk. She had seen Gray Beaver and his friends ride and train the many horses Keokuk had given to the Mesquakies. Now Gray Beaver turned his horse, and trotted it slowly up the hill.

Her heart pounded as he flipped the reins over his horse's head and let him graze freely nearby. It was not the way of their people for them to be alone. Gray Beaver walked slowly to Naosaqua and sat beside her. For a little while, there was silence.

Finally Gray Beaver said, "Many times I see you sitting up here on this hill. Are you troubled? What are your thoughts?"

"I am wondering how the earth can turn around," whispered Naosaqua, "and still be the same."

Gray Beaver looked puzzled. "I do not understand your words," he said.

Naosaqua took a deep breath. She would try to explain. "When the Mesquakie left Saukinek, they lost much. The crops had been burned, the happy days were left behind. The hard winter reached out with its icy hand and took many spirits." She paused for a moment and then went on. "Many bad things happened. Yet our people make new wickiups in the old way. Is there really a Forever Place or does it exist only in our hearts? Once more, spring has come and the crops are planted."

Gray Beaver's eyes had never left Naosaqua's face. "Naosaqua," he said gently, "did I now say this to you, one day in the hard winter, deep in the woods? The day that you made your prayer to the Spirit of the Woods and I followed you? Spring will always come, and crops will always be planted and grow for our people. Long after your spirit and mine have taken the Long Trail, the Mesquakie people will dance around the Ceremonial Fire to show the joy in their hearts for the earth and a good life."

Naosaqua's eyes blinked. So it had been Gray Beaver in the deep woods after all! He looked tenderly at her. He reached out and took hold of her two hands and held them, palms up.

"Think well on these words, my Naosaqua," he said. "In the one hand you hold your own destiny. Your future is for you to decide. In the other hand, you hold my destiny." He stopped speaking and looked straight into her eyes. Naosaqua could almost hear her heart beating. Gray Beaver continued softly, "It is for you to say if your two hands shall be put together." He held her two hands firmly in his own for a moment, and then with a slow sure movement, brought them both together. For the space of several heartbeats, they sat with their hands clasped, staring into each other's eyes.

Suddenly, Gray Beaver dropped her hands and strode away. Before Naosaqua could say a word, he was riding his horse slowly down the hill. He did not look back.

Naosaqua looked down at her hands. She could still feel the warmth of his hands on hers. Slowly, she put them together. "It is indeed as Old Grandmother said," she whispered to herself. "It will all work out if I listen to my heart." Her heart pounded in her breast.

Chapter 20

Naosaqua walked with Little Fawn through the grazing fields that surrounded the village. The time had come one full turn since the burning of the crops at Saukinek. Once again, they weeded the crops and looked forward to a good harvest. The horses were hobbled in the meadow they were passing. It was the First Moon of Flowering, the time the white man called June.

Little Fawn glanced slyly at Naosaqua. "I see Gray Beaver with the horses," she said. "Naosaqua, do you not see Gray Beaver with the horses?"

"I see him," Naosaqua answered quietly as she continued walking.

"We see him often," Little Fawn observed.

"Yes," Naosaqua agreed, "almost as often as Wind Rider. Did I not see him in our village just yesterday? Keokuk must have much business with our people to send him to us so many times. What does he do here?"

Little Fawn's eyes sparkled. "He does many things," she answered. "He brought much seed and corn for the planting of our crops."

"But that was early planting time," Naosaqua persisted. "What is it that pulls him back to our village so many times on his big black horse?"

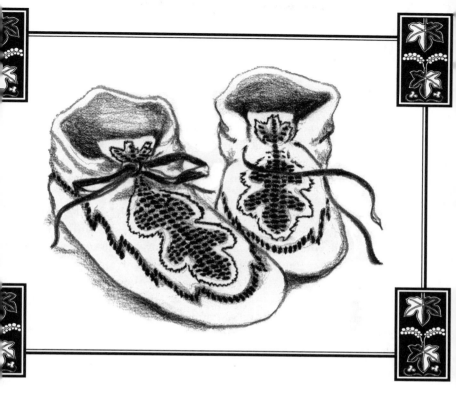

"He . . . he has many friends here," Little Fawn stammered. "Among Gray Beaver and his friends he has found many acquaintances to his liking. They trap and they ride. They ride mostly by the river."

"Where you just happen to be, gathering reeds for more mats," Naosaqua teased. "I had thought you were planning to make enough mats for the wickiup of every person in our tribe, Little Fawn!" She laughed.

"An abundance of reeds has never been a bad thing, Naosaqua!" Little Fawn exclaimed. Suddenly she stopped and grasped Naosaqua by the arm. "Is it not a good thing for his eye to fall upon me when he is here, Naosaqua?" she asked.

"I would say that is a good thing," Naosaqua answered. "Is it your wish that his eye be taken with you? I cannot help but know he is much in your thoughts, as he is much in your words, Little Fawn."

"Is it not the same with you and Gray Beaver?" Little Fawn asked shyly. "Long ago, White Cloud and I both knew that Gray Beaver would be playing his flute outside your wickiup when the First Moon of Flowering was right. But do you not wish his eye to fall upon you now, even through seasons will pass before you can share his wickiup? Is it not that way with you, Naosaqua?"

Naosaqua gazed into Little Fawn's eyes. "It is only that I consider you as close to my heart as a sister," she said slowly, "that I tell you this. His mother and my grandmother have spoken, and . . . and when he came with the small fire in a bowl in his hand . . ." she hesitated and then whispered, "I blew it out."

Little Fawn gazed at Naosaqua for a moment and then threw her arms wildly around her. "Oh, Naosaqua, Naosaqua," she cried, "I am so glad you told me!"

As they reached the edge of the village, Naosaqua said, "My father is returning this night. A runner came today. He said my father and the other hunters have been at Saukinek, trading." Her eyes shone. "I will be glad to see my father," she said. "I have a good feeling."

"I will leave you here," Little Fawn said. "It is time for my little brothers and sisters to be put into their sleeping places and I must help." She gazed at Naosaqua and then added, "Oh, my friend, I am much happy for you."

Naosaqua watched her friend leave and then turned and entered her wickiup. To her surprise, Red Arrow had already returned and was talking to Old Grandmother. They stopped talking and looked at her as she entered.

"How goes it with you, my daughter?" Red Arrow asked gently.

"Oh, Father," Naosaqua cried. "My heart sings because you are here. There were times I thought my eyes would never again behold your face!" She sat down next to her father as close as she could. She trembled at his nearness and her eyes filled with tears.

Red Arrow smiled at her. "How is it you do not ask if I have brought you a gift?" he asked.

"It is gift enough that you are here," Naosaqua answered.

Red Arrow pulled a parcel from within his blanket. "Then have I carried this over the trail for no one?" he asked.

Naosaqua said nothing. She could not believe this was like the old days when her father would always bring a gift for her and for Old Grandmother.

"This is for you, my mother," he said softly, turning to Old Grandmother. He laid a brightly colored shawl before O'Nokomess. "My heart rejoices that you are well and able to wear it." Old Grandmother did not say a thing. She picked up the gift and buried her face in its soft folds. Then slowly she drew it around her shoulders.

"And for you, my Naosaqua," said Red Arrow, "the one who walks in another's moccasins, let your feet now walk in your own moccasins on the path of the Mesquakies." Into Naosaqua's hands he put a beautiful pair of white moccasins, designed with flowers of blue and red beads. It was the Eastern Woodland motif, the emblem of the Mesquakies.

Naosaqua's hands quivered as she held her father's gift. Red Arrow looked at his daughter very seriously. "I have another gift for you," he said. "Give me your hand."

Naosaqua held out her hand to her father, palm upward. Into it Red Arrow placed three very small objects. They were the color of the sky on a bright blue day. They were the three blue beads she had left on her mother's grave at Saukinek.

"I think, my daughter," Red Arrow said softly, "they do not belong where I found them."

Naosaqua sat quietly, holding her new white moccasins in one hand and the three blue beads in the other. She looked from her father to her grandmother.

"I will retire to my sleeping place. Suddenly, I seem weary." She pillowed her head upon the white moccasins as she drew her sleeping robe about her, but she still held the three blue beads in her hand.

She watched as her father and grandmother also settled themselves comfortably in their sleeping robes. But sleep would not come to Naosaqua. She had a feeling her father and grandmother were not sleeping either although they lay very still and made no noise. A deep quiet filled the wickiup and in that quiet, Naosaqua heard it.

Slowly the sweet sound of a flute penetrated Naosaqua's wickiup. The music was filled with the sounds of the birds and small creatures from the woodlands. It spoke of good harvests and great hunts. It sang of Mesquakie life around a camp fire and of the two who would share that life.

Naosaqua rose slowly and pulled her buffalo sleeping robe around her. Quietly, she crossed the wickiup floor and went outside. Gray Beaver stood there, playing his flute for all to hear. She stood before him.

In her hand, she still held the three blue beads her father had brought her. In her heart, she felt her mother's spirit about her.

Listen to your heart, Old Grandmother had said. *It will work out.*

The music of Gray Beaver's flute fell upon Naosaqua's ears, sweeter than the song of any bird. Naosaqua gazed deeply into Gray Beaver's eyes and stood firm. Her heart beat steadily, like a small Mesquakie drum.

Mesquakie Calendar of Months

January . . . . Little Bear Moon
February . . . . Cold Moon of Winter
March . . . . Sap Moon
                  (Sugar Cane, Sugar Camps)
April. . . . . Fish Moon (Wild Fowl Shoot)
May . . . . Planting Moon
                  (food pits opened, crops planted,
                  fields cleaned)
June . . . . First Moon of Flowering
                  (young braves choose wives,
                  much feasting)
July. . . . . Mid-summer Moon
                  (big hunt for buffalo,
                  new canoes burned out)
August . . . . Elk Moon
September . . . . First Frosty Moon
October . . . . Rutting Moon
                  (feasts and visit other tribes)
November . . . . Turtle Moon
                  (new clothes and implements made)
December . . . . Big Bear Moon

About the Author

KATHERINE VON AHNEN is an award-winning poet and author of *Charlie Young Bear* (Roberts Rinehart, 1994), which received the first place award in historical fiction from the Wisconsin Regional Writers Association in 1987. She continues to write and works part-time at Cape May Point Lighthouse in New Jersey.

About the Artist

PAULETTE LIVERS LAMBERT has illustrated and designed many books for adults and children, among them *Evening: An Appalachian Lullaby* (Roberts Rinehart, 1995) and two books for The Council for Indian Education: *Quest for Courage* and *Navajo Long Walk* (Roberts Rinehart, 1994). She lives with her two daughters in Boulder, Colorado.

4741

If you liked *Heart of Naosaqua*, you'll like other books in The Council for Indian Education Series. Roberts Rinehart publishes books for all ages, both fiction and non-fiction, in the subjects of natural and cultural history, as well as picture books for young children. For more information about all of our books, please write or call for a catalog.

Roberts Rinehart Publishers
5455 Spine Road
Mezzanine West
Boulder, CO 80301
1-800-352-1985
In Colorado 530-4400